Recall the Earth

The Guardian Knights of Terra, Book Two

By Kyle Pratt

CAMDEN CASCADE

PUBLISHING

Recall the Earth
The Guardian Knights of Terra, Book Two
By Kyle Pratt

ISBN: 978-0-9983756-2-5
First Edition 1.0 – April 2017
All Rights Reserved

Editor: Ben Wolf
Cover Design: Inspired Cover Designs
This is a work of fiction. Names, characters, places, especially those on other planets, and incidents either are the product of the author's imagination or are used fictitiously, and any resemblance to actual persons, living or dead, events, or locales is entirely coincidental

Sign up for my no-spam monthly newsletter and get a free ebook.
Details are at the end of the novel.

Acknowledgements

Some authors write in relative isolation from a cabin in the woods or on the beach. I do not. I'm happy that there are people willing to take each of my chapters as they are written and give me honest feedback.

From the start, my wife Lorraine has been my encourager, first editor, critic, and beta-reader. She reads every chapter several times before anyone else sees it. Lorraine is also my office manager and business partner. Without her support, I would not be able to be an author.

I owe a huge debt of gratitude to Pat Thompson, Doyle McKim, Marcia Jacyna, and Jennifer Vandenberg for their critique of each chapter.

Finally, I appreciate Ben Wolf for his detailed editing of the manuscript and Jennifer Vandenberg for beta-reading the final draft just before it went to print.

Thank you!

Chapter 1

Prior system, Planet Delta

Cornet Lucas Baldwin awoke with a shudder. Pain radiated from every part of his body and declared that, at least for now, he lived. He blinked but saw only black. He tasted blood and wiped it with an unseen hand.

Reaching into the dark void, he felt nothing but air. He hung nearly upside down, still strapped into a seat.

He shook his head and blinked in the darkness as he struggled to recall what had happened. Screams of death and agony flowed into his consciousness. The Valac had attacked and taken planet Prior Delta. His marine unit had counterattacked, but a missile had hit his dart shortly after they entered the atmosphere. Their dart had crashed, leaving him upside down and still strapped to his seat.

Had anyone else lived? "Hello? Can anyone hear me?"

Silence.

He felt for the ethercomm button on his left sleeve and tapped the screen. "Assault command, this is first platoon." He tapped the screen again. It should've emanated a soft red glow. "Are you receiving me?"

Nothing.

In an attempt to release the straps he moved, but pain shot along his left arm like lightning. He moaned, and darkness overtook him.

When Lucas regained consciousness, he still hung upside down, but light filtered through the wreckage. Now he could see, but only with one eye. Blood stained the metal beneath him.

His blood. He winced.

Again he tried to call for help on the ethercomm. Again, the screen remained dark and he again heard nothing.

Several bodies hung from seats nearby. In the dim light, he spotted the remains of Mellor and Quin on one side and Farley on the other. Other corpses, torn and mutilated beyond recognition, lay strewn nearby. Why had he lived?

Lucas hung less than ten feet in the air but, with his injuries and the jagged metal of the hull, getting free would prove difficult. He eased his left arm forward but stopped when pain, like electrum bolts, shot along it.

With his right arm, Lucas grasped the harness and pressed the release. As his body dropped from the seat, he grabbed the belt with his good hand. The muscles in his arms and chest throbbed, but he now hung less than two feet from the ground. He slid down the strap and fell the last few inches.

Agonizing pain shot through his right leg. He collapsed. His right ankle was broken.

Using his good right arm and his unbroken left leg, Lucas crawled around the compartment checking any bodies that might possibly be alive. He discovered the torn, bloody body of Sergeant Collins near the rear of the craft.

He knew all of these men to varying degrees, but Collins had been more than just a soldier. Collins had helped and supported Lucas during every mission of his young career. Lucas slumped beside the sergeant's body and rested a hand on his shoulder. "May the God of Earth welcome you, my friend."

Lucas checked Collins's ethercomm. The familiar red glow appeared with a display in black letters and numbers. "Assault command … anybody on this web … this is Cornet Baldwin. Are you receiving me?"

Only silence returned to him. He pulled the module from the sergeant's suit and replaced his broken unit, being careful not to jar his injured arm. He slumped against the bulkhead and looked about the wrecked craft.

The smell of blood hung heavy around him. He had checked every body and confirmed that he alone had survived. His took a deep breath of death-filled air.

His head drooped to the side. A medicus bag lay nearby partially covered by debris. He crawled to it and injected himself with a painkiller and stimulant, drank water, and waited.

Minutes later, he felt much better. He cleaned and bandaged the wounds he could reach and splinted his right leg and ankle. Then he gathered more medical supplies, food, water, lances, and ammo.

After another set of injections, he used his good arm and leg to crawl through a hole in the dart with the supplies tied to a rope around his waist.

The light of the yellow Prior star revealed a world of barren rocks and hills. He scooped a handful of sand and gravel. So many good men had died for this tan and orange wasteland. Why?

He tried the ethercomm again. "Assault command … someone … this is Cornet Baldwin. Does anyone hear me?"

Perhaps it was the drugs, or venturing outside of the tomb the dart had become, but he continued to feel well. With the added light of the sun, Lucas performed a diagnostic on his combat suit. Nearly half the systems, including environment, chronometer, and stealth were down.

As the sun rose, it provided warmth, but as it continued its assent, it became a scorching blaze. He pulled himself to a spot of shade provided by the wreck.

This is where I'm going to die. He thought of his sister. They had argued many times, but he always knew that against anyone else, she would take his side. He hoped she'd marry someone she loved, not Prince Draven or the prince royal, and find happiness.

His thoughts drifted to Rachel—beautiful, bold, and dangerous with a battle lance. *Please, God of Earth, let her find the way home.*

He leaned his head against the hull. Death might come from dehydration, blood loss, or the Valac, but it would come.

The heat and fading stimulant made him drowsy. Lucas relaxed and allowed the darkness to embrace him.

An oppressive sun beat down from the sky when he awoke. He closed his eyes and shouted into the heavens, "God of Earth, why didn't I just die in the crash?"

A dart roared across the sky.

Lucas fumbled with the ethercomm controls. "Any station on this web, this is Cornet Lucas Baldwin of first platoon. I'm wounded and in need of assistance."

Only the breeze broke the silence.

Explosions thundered in the distance. Lucas smiled. If the fight still raged and humans had gained control of the planet, they would check this location for survivors. He might yet live.

Lucas drank more water and considered his options. He chuckled. With a broken leg and dislocated arm, he could barely move. Either other humans would find him or he would die. He clutched a battle lance, sat up, and watched the horizon.

As the sun moved across the sky, a black blotch appeared on a large rock outcrop about two-hundred yards ahead. Could it be a cave?

The monocular in his helmet revealed a shaded area but gave little indication of size.

It might provide a cooler, defensible position. For any searchers, he painted a message on the wreck using the only thing he had available at the moment: blood from one of his wounds. *In cave 200 yds N – Cornet Lucas.*

He drank another mouthful of water, injected himself once more, and then with the supplies still tied to his waist, he crawled toward the black spot.

The blazing sunlight and the dull misery from his drug-salved wounds soon overwhelmed his sense of time and distance. When he pulled himself the last few feet to the shade of the crevasse entrance, he slumped into limp semi-consciousness.

Later, he tried to move farther into the cool darkness, but slid down a steep slope into the cavity with his supplies clanging behind. He fell to a stop ten feet from the entrance and pain tore through him. Over the next few minutes, he pulled himself to a back corner of the grotto.

"Well, at least it's a bit cooler." He rubbed his sore head. "And defensible." Nothing remained but to stay alive and hope to be found by friends.

He injected more pain-killer but no stimulant. Gradually, his eyes closed.

He had no idea how long he slept. Dim light flowed from the cave entrance. Was it evening or morning? The temperature felt bearable. He drank a mouthful of water, shifted into a more comfortable position, and hoped it was morning. With the suit's environmental systems down, he didn't want to face a long, probably cold, night.

The light continued to fade.

Evening. Lucas sighed. Hours of darkness, cold, and pain lay ahead. Sleep closed his eyes.

Soft clicking sounds arose outside.

Lucas's eyes shot open.

The clicking grew more distinct, more familiar.

He grabbed a lance.

Valac were outside the cave.

*   *   *

Devon system, Onboard the Exeter Skylift

Rachel backed away from the men.

"Yes, Your Highness." The taller guard stepped closer to Katherine. "Kill the women and make it look like an accident."

The other guard grinned. "Happy to do this for you, Sire." He marched toward Naomi.

Prince Draven nodded. Then he turned and walked back into the skylift.

When the door slid closed behind the prince, the tall guard leapt for Katherine, but she dashed to the side.

Naomi sprinted toward the dart.

Rachel ran to help Katherine but crashed into the guard chasing Naomi. They fell to the deck in a tangle of arms and legs.

The man grabbed Rachel's foot.

Katherine kicked his head.

Rachel stood and kicked him in the groin. With Katherine, she ran for the dart.

The remaining two guards raced behind them.

Rachel entered first by a stride.

As Katherine lunged in, she slapped a nearby control panel. The door slid shut.

The taller guard's face contorted, and he banged his fist against the portal.

"That'll only give us a few seconds." Katherine breathed hard and fast. She tapped the band on her wrist. "Naomi, go to the bridge and launch the dart."

"Ahhhh …" Naomi's hesitant voice emanated from the bracelet.

"I'll be right there." Katherine turned to Rachel. "Follow me."

Rachel followed Katherine down an ornate passageway of granite floors, wood panels and portrait paintings.

"That's the bridge." Without looking back at Rachel, Katherine pointed to a hatch yards ahead.

Footfalls thundered behind Rachel. A fist slammed into her back. She stumbled and fell against the bulkhead.

The shorter guard stepped over her and grabbed Katherine's hair. Using his other arm, he swung at Katherine's face.

She blocked the first blow, but not the second.

The dart shuddered.

The taller guard hurried down the passageway.

Rachel stumbled as she stood. It felt like a plane lifting into the air. Then she floated.

Weightless? She struggled not to vomit.

A hand lance hung from the belt of the short guard, who continued to beat Katherine. Rachel swam and pulled herself toward him.

The short guard braced his feet against the bulkhead.

Katherine floated away.

When Rachel floated closer, the man spotted her and punched her in the face.

Spiraling away due to the blow, Rachel still managed to grab the lance.

The guard turned and grabbed for the weapon.

Rachel fired several shots.

Blood streamed toward Rachel as the man's body drifted away.

Katherine drifted limp in the air.

Her heart pounding, Rachel swam to her. Katherine's nose lay limp to one side. Angry red bruises surrounded swollen eyes. Her lips and nose bled into the air.

Rage boiled inside Rachel. She had killed one guard. She would kill the other.

Rachel grabbed Katherine by the arm and used door handles, picture frames and edges to pull them along the passageway. At a junction with another passageway, they passed the body of the short guard.

Ahead, Rachel heard a lance fire, and the other guard shouted, but as she moved toward the noise, she drifted toward the deck. *Gravity? Weight?*

Katherine thumped to the deck like a dropped sack.

The nose of the craft tilted down.

Rachel slid several inches forward.

She tried, but couldn't budge Katherine. Doubt coursed through her. Should she help Naomi or stay with Katherine? "God, protect Katherine." Rachel left her and ran forward with the lance in hand. She burst into the largest bridge she had seen. "Where's the man?"

Naomi sat in the pilot seat working controls. Three other seats were arranged in a semi-circle on either side of her. An elongated view screen stood before all the positions.

Naomi didn't turn from the controls. "I shot at him. He ran. We have another problem—I don't know how to fly this dart." She pointed to the screen. "Look!"

The ground raced closer.

Naomi glanced over her shoulder. "Do you know how to … Watch out!"

Rachel ducked and turned.

The tall guard, wearing a bloodstained shirt, stood at the entrance to the bridge, with a lance in-hand. He raised it.

Rachel fired first, and the man collapsed in a blood-red heap.

"We're going to crash." Naomi shook her head. "I—I don't know what to do!"

Rachel's heart pounded. She stared at Naomi and then at the view screen. Snowcapped mountains raced toward them.

A thud behind Rachel caused her to turn her head.

Katherine stumbled over the body and fell to her knees in the doorway. Blood ran down her face. "Naomi, Rachel? Help me. I can't see."

Rachel ran to her. Katherine's eyes were swollen shut. Her nose and several teeth wobbled with each move of her head. "Come with me. I'll strap you in."

"Are you okay?" Katherine grabbed Rachel's arms. "Is Naomi unharmed? What about the men? Did we get away from them?"

"Yes to all of those." Rachel sat Katherine down and strapped her in.

"Why are we descending so fast?"

"Because helots don't receive flight training!" Naomi shouted.

Rachel sat and strapped herself in.

"Fire forward and lower thrusters." Katherine pointed an unsteady hand toward the flight controls. "Red slider. Pull the nose up."

"I'm trying!" Naomi's hands sped along the controls. She turned to Katherine. "What else can I do?"

The dart slammed into the ground.

Chapter 2

Prior system, Planet Delta

Lucas snapped his helmet in place. Sweat and fear permeated him. With both stealth and environmental systems of his suit malfunctioning, it wouldn't take long for the Valac to sniff him out.

He aimed the battle lance at the cave entrance. As he waited, a plan came to mind. It probably wouldn't save him, but it would allow him to kill many of the enemy before they reached him.

The clicking sound grew closer.

Shadows danced outside the cave.

Lucas waited.

The scorpion-like mandibles of a Valac swayed in the entrance. Its tongue thrust in and out, tasting the smells in the air.

Lucas waited.

A Valac roar reverberated through Lucas's body. Then it charged.

Lucas fired as the bulk of the creature filled the opening.

It dropped, blocking more than half the entrance.

Other Valac pulled the body away.

Another charged, and died.

Shadows and low-pitched growls intimated more Valac just out of sight.

Lucas considered using explosives, but they'd either bury him alive inside the grotto or blast the opening and create a larger way in for the Valac.

Before they could act, Lucas fired heat-seeking rounds through the hole, followed by a fragbomb.

Multiple roars and cries filled his ears. The stench of Valac blood hung in the air.

Lucas grinned as he imagined the carnage outside. "I'm Cornet Lucas Nathaniel Alexander Baldwin," he shouted. "I'm going to make you pay dearly for my life!"

A deep baritone rumble shook him. The stone before him cracked and splintered.

This was more than his little explosive round.

The front wall of the grotto collapsed.

Dozens of Valac poured over the rubble.

Lucas fired again and again as the monsters raced toward him.

The Valac launched stingers that tore into his arms.

Lucas thought he heard lance fire in the distance as he slipped into darkness. *Late. You're too late.*

*   *   *

Devon system, Planet Exeter

The Valac song faded from Rachel's mind as she awoke to a dim, shadow-filled world of torn metal, debris, and unfamiliar voices. It felt as if she hung by straps from the ceiling. Someone pressed against her chest, and she fell into a man's arms.

"We need to hurry," a voice in the darkness urged. "The atomic generator is overheating. The cooling system is failing and when it does, it'll explode."

A man with dark eyes and wearing a black suit with a stiff, high collar leaned close to Rachel. "This one's eyes are open, but she looks dead. How is Lady Katherine?"

"Not well." Naomi's voice came from somewhere in the darkness. "Hurry, please."

"They're both weak," another man said. "They may perish in route to Camden."

"Pray they do not." Naomi said. "For my sake, for all our sakes."

Darkness engulfed Rachel.

Pain stirred her to consciousness some unknown time later. Her chest, shoulders, arms and legs all throbbed, but she had a buoyant, floating sensation.

Beside the bed, a cart with a computare display beeped softly as numbers scrolled down the screen and disappeared. She guessed that the red tabs on her chest monitored her body and that one up-and-down line on the display represented her heartbeat.

A door slid open, and soft lights came on.

A man with gray hair entered, and smiled at her. He wore a military uniform like those Lucas, Tybalt, and others had worn on the warship, but she didn't recognize him.

Through the pain she struggled to speak in her best Lingua Terra. "Where am I?"

The man tapped on the screen. "Just rest. You'll have answers later."

Rachel drifted to sleep.

Green patterns swayed back and forth on white walls when she next awoke. Rachel turned her head toward the warm light that poured in through partially open balcony doors. Lacy shamrock curtains arched to the sides and continued to the floor.

From her bed, she gazed outside into a clear dark blue sky. The tops of trees were visible in the distance but not the ground.

She lay in a large bed of soft white sheets and a forest green comforter. Again, she felt the sensation of floating. Two chairs and a small table stood along the far wall under paintings of country scenes. Large rugs covered hardwood floors.

A door frame on her right contained only a blank wall with no knobs or key holes. How would anyone enter? Was this an ornate prison?

As if in answer to her question, the white panel within the door frame slid to the side with a soft whoosh.

The same gray-haired man she'd seen earlier walked in. Again, he smiled at her. "Are you feeling better?" He carried a chair to the side of the bed and sat beside her.

"Yes." Rachel nodded. "Where am I?"

"You're at Camden, the summer estate of the Marquis of Devon." He picked up a palmcomp from the cart and tapped on it.

She sighed with relief, recalling that Camden had been their destination. "How long have I been here?"

"Five days."

Rachel struggled to put her thoughts in order. "We were in a crash! Is Katherine okay?"

"Lord Baldwin's daughter?" the man asked. "She's recovering in the next room."

"I'd like to speak with her."

"She remains unconscious." He glanced at the display and tapped again on the palmcomp. "You have a most peculiar accent. From where do you come?"

That question brought to mind the last man in uniform who had smiled at her. He'd tried to kill her because of where she came from. Her stomach churned; her heart pounded. "I'm tired."

"Rest, then." He tapped some notes into a palmcomp and replaced it on the cart. "I'll be back later."

After he left, she lifted herself into a sitting position and rested her back against the headboard. She needed to see Katherine, confirm that she was nearby, and hopefully talk to her.

Rachel swung her legs over the edge of the bed and sat up. She took a few moments to flex her stiff and sore limbs. All of them worked; nothing was broken or dislocated. Then she pulled back the thin white robe, revealing additional red tabs and deep purple and green bruises that wrapped around her arms, legs, and chest. With slow and careful movement, she eased her feet to the floor.

As she rose from the bed, she felt heavier but dismissed it as having lain there too long. Taking small steps and using her hands to steady herself, she walked through the door onto the balcony.

The one wall of the building she could see looked like a brownstone English mansion. She gazed in all directions, but couldn't see a door to the house or a road. This appeared to be the side or back of the house.

Snow-covered mountains rose high on her left. Low in the sky a yellow sun shined in a deep blue sky. It was either early morning or late in the evening. Or did such things work differently on this planet?

To her right, the terrain sloped toward a distant sea. Lush green lawns and gardens covered acres before her. Rachel continued to take in the beautiful setting and marveled at being on some distant planet.

But was it an alien world? Trees, green grass, and blue sky—it all looked Earth-like. For several moments, she stood confused.

In the distance, a tiny spot appeared in the sky and moved like an airplane to her left. Then it seemed to stop, and gradually grow larger, until she identified it as a dart with wings extended. Even as it approached the house, the craft flew without a sound. Only when it neared the mansion did its thrusters fire with a roar. The wings retracted and it appeared to land on the roof of the building.

Okay, this is an alien world, and I need to get out of the room.

Rachel looked down and then up. Two floors were below her, one above. With no fire escape or convenient ivy vining along the wall, escape via the balcony seemed unlikely.

She hurried across the room as fast as her sore muscles would allow, and examined the door. If she hadn't seen it slide open for the doctor, she would've thought it part of the wall.

But I've seen it open. She ran her hand along the edges, pushing, pulling, and probing. "So, this is a prison. I need to leave, but there's no way out."

"The automatos controls of the door are set to remain closed," a familiar female voice announced. "However, I can change them and open the door, if you wish."

Just as when she heard it on Katherine's ship, the voice seemed to come from all around.

Light shimmered behind her. "Is that what you wish?"

Rachel spun around. A girl, about her own age, with long brunette hair, stood behind her. Rachel stumbled back against the wall. "Wish? How did you get in? Who are you?"

The girl's image shimmered slightly. Dust particles in the air passed through her.

Could this be the voice I heard on Katherine's ship? "Are you Sarah?"

"Yes."

Rachel stepped close to the image and examined it carefully. "I thought you were just a program on Katherine's ship."

"I am an intelligent automatos. I follow Katherine using public and Baldwin family web systems. That way I can be of greater service. And Lady Katherine instructed me to be of service while you were her guest."

"Thank you." Rachel continued her examination. "Why didn't you appear when we were aboard the *Lady Katherine*?"

"The ship has only one holoview, in the foyer." Sarah turned as Rachel walked around her. "And no need to use the foyer occurred while you were aboard the ship."

Rachel stepped back and smiled. "I look forward to learning more about you, but for now, please open the door."

"Yes, Madame." Sarah curtsied. The door slid away and Rachel followed Sarah into a wide hallway. Along the walls hung paintings of men in uniforms, women in regal dresses, and country scenes.

"Where's Katherine?"

Sarah pointed, leading her down the hall, flickering as she did. At the doorway of the room, Sarah disappeared.

Rachel ran into the room and found Sarah just inside.

"Please enter. Katherine is there, in bed." Again, she pointed.

Rachel ran to her friend's side. Katherine lay in a similar bed, with a pastel blue comforter. The swelling had decreased around her eyes, but large purple and green bruises remained on much of her face. Still staring at her friend, Rachel spoke to Sarah. "Is she recovering? Will she be okay?"

"Yes." Sarah stepped near the bed. "Yes."

Rachel expected more details but quickly realized her questions had been answered in full and no additional information would be forthcoming.

She resolved to stay near until Katherine awoke. Rachel pulled a chair to the bed, sat down and, for the first time, looked about. Both rooms had balconies, chairs, small tables, and rugs, but green colors styled Rachel's room; this nearly identical one had hues of blue.

As Rachel considered her situation, a profound sense of loneliness and fear weighed upon her. Katherine, her only friend on this strange new world, lay comatose. She had no idea where Lucas, Tybalt, or Konrad might be, and some cowardly Prince wanted her dead. Tears welled in her eyes. Then a new thought came to mind. "Where is Katherine's lady's maid ... uh, Naomi?"

Sarah stood near the middle of the room with her head tilted slightly. "The lady's maid Naomi has been arrested."

"When?"

"Four minutes ago."

Bang. Thud.

Rachel ran to the window and looked out. "What's going on?"

Men in black uniforms and carrying battle lances stood guard facing the house.

Rachel turned to Sarah. "Who are these guys?"

"They are Nightwatch, the enforcement arm of Star Chamber," Sarah said without emotion. "They are here to arrest you."

Chapter 3

Devon system, Planet Exeter

"Arrest me?" Rachel slumped to her knees, still facing Katherine. Arrest might be better than being beaten to death, but either way she feared death would be the result.

Sarah flickered. "Nightwatch is asking the house systems for your location."

"Do you have to tell them?"

"Not if you don't wish it."

"No, I don't wish it." Rachel spun around. "Lie to them. How can I get out of the house and hide somewhere?"

"All exits are guarded. The house is surrounded."

Fear roiled within Rachel. "Ah …." *What can I do? Where can I go?* "Sarah, what's the most secluded spot in the building?"

The computare projection grinned. "The cellar has several rarely used rooms."

"Show me." Rachel placed a hand on the bed to stand, but instead pressed against Katherine's arm.

Her friend moaned.

Rachel slumped back to her knees as she recalled her resolution to stay by Katherine.

Sarah flickered and disappeared.

Had Nightwatch taken control of Sarah? Rachel stroked Katherine's bruised face. Prince Draven and his men would soon burst into the room and kill them both.

No. She wouldn't let that happen. She needed to find a way to protect her friend. "Sarah, are there any lances in the house?"

Sarah didn't answer or reappear.

A mixture of frustration and fear swirled within Rachel. She sighed and buried her face in Katherine's blanket. Escape seemed impossible. Fighting seemed impossible. She believed in God, but had never felt particularly religious, but prayer now seemed like the only option. She bent over Katherine's bedside and searched for words.

"God … uh, I really need your help. I don't understand why Prince Draven wants Katherine and me dead. I didn't do anything wrong. Now all these people are in danger, and it feels like my fault."

The now-familiar flicker of Sarah brightened the room. Wanting to speak with her, Rachel rushed her prayer. "Please, keep me safe. Let Katherine live. Keep her safe. And wherever Lucas is, keep him safe, also." Thoughts of Konrad and Tybalt came to her. "Uh, keep everyone safe. Amen."

Rachel spun around to greet Sarah.

Near the center of the room the holo image of a man stood. He looked about forty, or maybe a few years older with gray dotting his brown hair and beard. Despite his age, he appeared lean and muscular in his uniform. A hand lance hung from his belt.

Rachel gasped.

The man flashed and disappeared.

"Sarah?" Rachel stumbled backward. Fear churned within her.

The door whooshed open.

The same bearded man she'd seen as a halo image walked into the room.

Rachel doubled her fists and assumed the stance of a boxer.

A slight grin crept onto the man's face. "I am Lord Admiral Farold Baldwin, the Marquis of Devon. I'm not here to harm you."

"Oh!" Rachel recognized the name of Katherine and Lucas' father. She relaxed her stance, but then remembered she wore only a thin robe. She pulled it tight, trying to think of what she should do next. "Uhhhhh."

Sarah reappeared and curtsied.

Rachel followed Sarah's example and curtsied, but swayed as she did.

"Nightwatch has sequestered all household staff to the servant's hall," Sarah advised. "They are moving toward this wing of the house. Your personal guard is in the hallway. A battalion of marines will arrive in less than fifteen minutes."

"Thank you, Sarah." Farold folded his arms. "Continue to spy on Nightwatch and jam their communications. Advise me when they begin searching this wing of the house and when the marines arrive."

"Yes, Lord Devon." Sarah stood still, but her eyes widened.

Farold's arms lowered to his side as he turned to Rachel. "Yesterday, when I arrived back on Exeter, Naomi told me that a friend fought beside them against three attackers. Katherine awoke briefly later that day and confirmed much of what she said."

Rachel glanced at the unconscious Katherine.

"Then, moments ago, I used Sarah to see into this room and found you praying for the safety of both Katherine and Lucas. I assume that you are the friend who fought beside Katherine and Naomi?"

"Yes, sir."

"Then you are indeed her friend—and mine."

He pulled a chair beside Katherine's bed. "Sit with me, child, and tell me everything, but do so quickly, for we have little time. Nightwatch has invaded my home."

Rachel sat beside him, pulled the robe tight around her, and poured out her story from her last memory on Earth, to her torture by the Auxilum, and the battle that freed her.

As she spoke, Farold's gaze remained fixed on Katherine.

Rachel told of seeing a young man, but left out the fact that she was naked at the time. "That was your son, Lucas. I asked for help, but he shot me." Rachel realized what she'd just said. She shook her head. "I don't blame him. He must've had a good reason. There's so much I still don't understand."

"A most inauspicious meeting." Farold grinned. "You don't know why he shot you?"

"No." She shook her head. "I'm not sure. Right before he did it, I killed one of the last Aux."

"I see." Farold nodded. "I wouldn't share that fact with anyone else. Continue your story."

She told of waking in jail on the ship.

"Brig." Farold corrected. "A jail on a ship is called the brig."

"Oh. There're a lot of words in your language that I'm still learning. Well, I wasn't out of that brig for long when the Valac attacked the ship. That's when I first met Prince Draven." Rachel described their mutual encounter with the enemy. "He's not much of a fighter."

"No, he's not."

"I shot more of the Valac, than he did, but another time they sang to me."

"The Valac sang to you?"

She nodded.

Sarah stepped forward. "Excuse me, my Lord. Nightwatch is on the first floor of this wing."

"I believe I've heard enough of your story for now. Follow me." Farold squeezed his daughter's hand, stood, and marched to the door. It opened as he neared.

Rachel followed him into a hall crowded with men armed with battle lances and dressed in similar uniforms to what Lucas had worn.

"First squad, stay here and guard this room. Allow no one entry," Farold ordered. "Second squad with me. Sarah, take the lead and report any activity."

Rachel looked back to see Sarah disappear and then reappear ahead of the squad.

The group passed more than a dozen doors, and as many paintings, as they continued down the hallway, around a corner, and along another hall.

"The marines have arrived," Sarah advised. "The battalion commander wishes to speak with you." Her image flashed and turned into a man in uniform.

"What are your orders, Admiral?"

"Cover all the Nightwatch soldiers. Shoot any that fire upon you."

The officer pursed his lips. "I have word Prince Draven is leading this … uh, incursion."

"Draven is not your concern." Farold scowled. "Do as I order."

"Yes, sir." The man disappeared.

Sarah reappeared, and everyone continued along the hall toward a bannister.

A silver and blue ball, about the size of a basketball, flew up the stairs and along the hallway. Red beams radiated from the device, and touched every surface as it proceeded toward them.

"My Lord, a survey craft is—"

"I can see it, Sarah," Farold snarled.

Rachel blinked as a beam swiped her face.

It stopped about ten yards away. "Rachel, of unknown family, you are under arrest by order of Star Chamber. Do you surrender?"

Farold pulled the hand lance from his belt and shot the ball. Pieces flew into the walls, ceiling, and floor.

"No, she does not surrender." Farold stepped over a smoldering chunk, and continued down the hall.

Rachel and the soldiers hurried to catch up. She followed them down the stairs. Below, a foyer on the main floor came into view.

The room looked to be half the size of her home on Earth. Two hallways connected to it, and mammoth double doors stood directly ahead. Columns, paintings, and busts on pedestals lined the walls.

As Rachel stepped into the foyer, she spotted a bigger-than-life painting of Farold on one side of a door and a woman about his age on the other.

A vaguely familiar man in a dark suit and stiff high collar stepped through the large doors. "Excuse me sir," he said to Farold. "Prince Draven is here to see you."

Soldiers in black burst into the room from the side halls and through the doors.

The marines with Farold encircled him and Sarah.

For a moment the two groups stared at each other.

"Why are you in my home?" Farold stepped forward, out of the ring of marines, and growled.

The large doors opened again. The Nightwatch soldiers stirred and parted as Prince Draven marched to the center of the room.

Everyone snapped to attention.

Farold stepped closer to him and bowed.

"Turn the provocateur over to me," Prince Draven commanded, "and this night will end peacefully."

Chapter 4

Devon system, Planet Exeter

"Who are you calling a provocateur, Your Highness?" Farold asked. "This girl that you ordered beaten to death, or my daughter, still convalescing from the torture your Nightwatch villains inflicted upon her in their murder attempt?"

Murmurs rose among the men.

Prince Draven sucked in a long breath. "I would prefer to speak of this privately."

"I would prefer to speak of this publicly. Sarah, record and send to all the vid outlets."

"Yes, my Lord," answered Sarah's omnipresent voice.

For a moment, the world seemed to freeze as two lines of men stared at each other across the room.

"I will return in the morning," Prince Draven snarled. "At that time you will receive me—alone."

Again, Farold bowed. "Your Highness is always welcome in my home. No need to knock."

The prince marched from the room, followed by the Nightwatch soldiers.

When Draven and his men were gone, Farold ordered Sarah to stop recording and then huddled with the marines to discuss security.

Rachel's bruised legs ached, and the couch in the corner of the foyer beckoned her so she lowered herself onto the velvet cushions. Men strode back and forth, but everyone ignored her. She leaned against the cold stone wall and closed her eyes.

The conversations faded to background noise as exhaustion swept over her. In seconds, she'd fall asleep right there in the foyer, wearing only her hospital robe. She didn't care.

Nearby, a man coughed.

A moment later he coughed again.

Rachel grudgingly opened one eye. Before her stood the same vaguely familiar man she'd seen in the foyer moments earlier. His dark eyes and suit contrasted with his gray hair. She had seen him somewhere before tonight, but where? It took a moment to put the bits of memory together. After the dart crash, when she lingered between consciousness and darkness, she had seen him in this same black suit high collar.

"Lady Devon requests your presence."

"Me?"

He nodded.

"You carried me out of the dart after the crash."

Again, he nodded. "We should not keep Lady Devon waiting."

Rachel followed him across the foyer.

"Thank you for helping me." Side-by-side, they climbed the staircase. "Uh, what's your name?"

"I am Alton, the head butler." They reached the landing, and he gestured left.

"You wore a dark suit when you carried me from the crash."

"You were more awake than I believed at the time." They turned a corner and headed down another hallway.

"But now you're in uniform."

"Yes, all men have been called to service. The situation is dire. The Valac have taken a dozen worlds."

Rachel looked down and bit her lip. Why had Prince Draven spent so much time trying to kill or arrest her and Katherine if the situation was so bad? She considered asking Alton, but she didn't know what he knew, and she had no desire to increase her notoriety.

Alton stopped and pressed his hand to a door. A soft glow surrounded it and then faded.

A woman's voice said, "Enter."

The door slid aside.

Alton stepped back. "Miss Rachel to see you, Lady Devon." He motioned for Rachel to enter.

She stepped in, and the door closed with Alton outside.

Across the room, in a plush, burgundy upholstered chair with carved wooden legs and arms, sat a woman. Her auburn hair gently curled to her waist. She had dark eyes and fair skin. In another time and place, she might've been a Viking queen sitting on her throne. Rachel recognized her as the woman in the bigger-than-life painting in the foyer of the mansion.

"I am Lady Devon." She extended her arm toward a nearby chair. "Please sit. I've wanted to meet the young woman who has thrown this household into so much turmoil."

"I'm sorry. I didn't want any of this." Rachel considered what to say next. Farold had probably told his wife what he knew or suspected, but she decided to be careful. "I'd just like to return home."

Lady Devon nodded. "I hope we can help you with that goal." She picked up a glass of what looked like water and took a sip. "Naomi, my daughter's lady's maid, spoke highly of you. During a brief period of consciousness, Katherine did also, and she added some most extraordinary details."

Unable to figure out what to say, Rachel remained silent.

"Did you speak with my husband, Lord Devon?"

"Farold?"

A grin spread across the woman's face. "Yes."

Rachel nodded.

"Then your presence here means you remain a guest in our home. Dr. Meredith tells me you made a good recovery. Perhaps we can get those medtabs off and some more appropriate clothing on you."

That moment, a woman and two girls about Rachel's age entered with multiple gowns, a corset, petticoat, shoes and other clothing items she couldn't name.

From her seat Lady Devon gestured to the dresses. "These are Katherine's gowns from last season."

Rachel stepped to the girls and examined the dresses. "They look very Victorian."

"Victorian?" Lady Devon asked.

"Uh ...." Rachel sucked in a breath. "It's just a word for ... beautiful." She wanted to change the subject. "What happened to the dress from the shop on the skylift?"

"That was torn and mangled in the crash." Lady Devon pointed to a forest green dress with white lace. "Show us that one."

The woman tapped on a palmcomp.

"Would you move in front of the glass, Miss?" One of the younger servant girls, a blonde, pointed to a large full-length mirror.

Rachel did as directed, recalling the mirror from the skylift store, and she gritted her teeth. Her hair needed serious combing, and while the robe stretched longer than those from Earth, it didn't look any better.

The reflection fluttered. The green gown replaced the horrid robe in the mirror.

Rachel moved back and forth and turned around. Hoping to curtail the fashion review with her as the model, she said, "This is lovely."

More than an hour passed before Lady Devon nodded approval. By that time, with the practiced precision of the girls, the magic of the mirror, and advice from Lady Devon, they transformed Rachel from a girl with frazzled hair and wearing a thin linen robe into an elegant lady—from another time period. She wore an ankle-length blue dress trimmed with delicate cream lace over a tight, but flexible, corset.

"I'll have the furnishings in your room changed from medical to something more comfortable." Lady Devon beamed. "Anna will be your lady's maid."

The blonde girl curtsied. "Yes, Lady Devon."

Rachel wanted to protest that she didn't need a maid, but then realized she had no idea how to find anything in the house. She smiled at Anna.

Lady Devon stood. "You may all go."

The servants curtsied.

Rachel clumsily followed their example and then turned to Anna. "Can you lead me back to my room?"

Anna grinned. "Follow me, Miss." As they stepped into the hallway, she said, "We're in the south wing of the house. Your room is in the north. If you're ever lost, just ask one of the servants or Sarah."

Rachel's bruised legs struggled to keep up with Anna.

"Do, you have a bracelet?" Anna pointed to Rachel's wrist.

"No. I must've lost it in the crash." That was a lie, but a believable one.

"I'll ask Alton to have a new one made for you."

By the time they reached her room, it had been transformed. The medical cart had disappeared, and a carved, four-poster bed had replaced the hospital-style bed. A dresser, two chairs and a couple of small tables had also been added.

"Very nice." Rachel turned slowly as she looked over the new furnishings. Her stomach grumbled with hunger. "Perhaps I could wash up and get some—"

The lights dimmed and turned red.

An alarm wavered.

Anna gasped. "The Valac are attacking the Devon system."

Chapter 5

Devon System, Planet Exeter

No blasts or explosions thundered, and all seemed peaceful after the alarms quit. Rachel stared at Anna, seeking advice or direction, but Anna stepped to the bed and pulled back the sheets.

Rachel hurried onto the balcony and scanned the horizon. The night seemed quiet, but dozens of darts crisscrossed in the air. Others took off nearby. "Should we go to a bomb shelter?"

"A blast shelter?" Anna fluffed the pillow. "We never have before. Shall I turn on the vids?"

Stepping back in to the room, Rachel looked for a TV screen. "Uh … sure. Where are they?"

Anna grinned, and then turned and faced the blank wall across from the bed. "Sarah, display news vids."

Six screens appeared on the plain white wall. But this wasn't television. It seemed like a half dozen holographic windows had opened. The voices overlapped.

"How do you watch six?"

Anna giggled. "Pick one."

Rachel pointed.

"Sarah, silence all but vid two."

"… Valac have broken through the outer defense perimeter," a newscaster in military uniform declared. "All soldiers, marines, and sailors report to their stations."

The newscaster continued to talk over vids of darts launching into the sky and spaceships shooting into Mage Tunnels. "Units of the Orion fleet will soon reinforce the outer defense ring."

Rachel sat on the bed and continued to watch, but the announcers and reporters provided little actual information.

Rachel gestured toward the balcony door. "If they're attacking Devon, why can't I see it?"

"The Valac are attacking the Devon system. Exeter is just one planet in that system, and many ships and brave men stand between them and us."

Chimes preceded Sarah's voice. "A maid is at the door."

Anna collected an armful of clothing from the maid. "Sarah, open the closet."

A doorway opened in the wall beside the bed and Anna disappeared within. When she returned, her gaze sank to the floor. "May I ask a question?"

"Of course."

"When you crashed, Naomi called the staff here at Camden House for help. She said you were the Daughter of Earth. And, when Katherine awoke for a few minutes yesterday, two lady's maids were in the room. She said similar surprising things about you."

Fear permeated Rachel. She knew what Anna was about to ask..

Anna pursed her lips. "Are you the Daughter of Earth?"

Rachel had little desire to lie to Anna, but she had less desire to tell the truth. Rachel knew that helots looked to her as a savior from their plight, and she guessed that Anna was one, but being from Earth had nearly gotten her arrested and killed. For reasons she didn't fully understand, the authorities considered her, and the existence of Earth, a threat.

She stared at Anna and sighed. It seemed Anna already knew much of her story. Rachel sucked in a deep breath. "I'm not the Daughter of Earth, just an average teenage girl … from Earth."

Anna's eyes widened and a smile parted her lips. "Naomi and Katherine both believe there is greatness within you."

"Greatness?" Rachel shook her head. "There's nothing special about me."

Anna shrugged. "Sometimes greatness is thrust upon us."

"And sometimes you're just a teenage girl."

For several minutes, Rachel lounged on the bed and Anna sat in a chair as they watched the vids.

Rachel's stomach grumbled. "Where can I get some food in this house?"

"Dinner has long passed, but I could have something brought up from the kitchen."

"That would be nice."

Anna summoned Sarah and ordered food, and then she turned to Rachel with a frown. "Please Miss, tell no one I asked those questions."

Rachel heard fear in the girl's voice. "Are you a helot ... a Seeker of Earth?"

Anna nodded.

"Rest assured, I won't be talking about this."

Several minutes later, Sarah announced a footman at the door with food.

Anna hurried to the door.

As he passed the tray to Anna, the footman stepped in the doorway.

Rachel turned toward the movement and made eye contact with him—a young teenage boy.

Anna used the tray to push him out and then set the food beside Rachel on the bed.

"Have you eaten?" Rachel asked as she chewed on the first bite of a sweet purple vegetable.

"Yes, earlier with the other servants."

"Are all of the servants Seekers?"

"Yes, except Alton, the head butler."

"Good to know." When she had finished eating, Rachel yawned. "I'm tired. Could you help me out of this dress and corset?"

She smiled. "That's one of my duties."

The vids still played on the wall, but Rachel lay in the bed and closed her eyes, just to rest them for a moment.

*   *   *

Sarah announced that Anna waited at the door.

"Uhhh ... enter." Rachel sat up and tried to shake a dream of Valac singing from her head as the door opened.

"Good morning. Miss." Anna bounded in carrying a palmcomp and a bracelet. "Sarah, open curtains and closet." She turned to Rachel as light poured into the room. "Did you want the vids on?"

"Morning?" Rachel squinted. "Are we winning the battle?"

"Perhaps the battle. The Valac have been pushed from the Devon system, but fighting continues around Efford, Prior, Phoenix—"

"No vids." Rachel sat up, and rubbed her eyes.

"I need to dress you and configure your new bracelet. You have a busy schedule today."

"I do?"

Anna nodded.

"Why? What am I going to be doing?"

"Katherine awoke last night, so I'm sure you'll want to visit her, and—"

"Oh, yes, absolutely." Rachel stood. "Let's go now."

"The doctors and family are with her." Anna looked at the palmcomp. "Breakfast is in thirty minutes; afterward you have a meeting with Lord Baldwin—"

"Farold? I'm meeting with him?"

"Yes." Anna giggled. "Shall we get you dressed?"

"Sure."

She walked toward the closet still staring at the display in her hand. "And then Lord Baldwin wants you available for the meeting with Prince Draven."

Rachel's stomach churned at the mention of the prince.

Anna disappeared into the closet. When she emerged seconds later, she held a pastel green dress. "And … well, if you can. Naomi is a friend of mine, of all the servants really, could you please have her freed?"

"I can't … I don't have any power."

"You will."

Anger stirred in Rachel. "Not now, I don't. I'm just trying to stay alive."

"Yes." Anna looked at the floor. "Sorry, miss. Let's get you dressed."

When Rachel was fully dressed, Anna slipped the bracelet onto Rachel's wrist, and it shrank to a snug fit. Then it warmed, and Rachel felt a pinch.

Anna tapped on the palmcomp. "The bracelet has the guest configuration for Camden House. You'll be able to open most doors, summon Sarah, or summon me."

"Thank you. Please show me to breakfast."

A footman served the meal in a dining room the size of a school classroom. Rachel sat alone at a massive wooden table with fourteen seats.

The footman stood in the corner and stared across the room.

What exactly is a footman? Does he have big feet? She glanced at him, but he turned away.

The head butler, Alton, had greeted her at the door and explained that Lord and Lady Baldwin had eaten earlier and were now with Katherine. He added that Victor and Lucas were still off-planet.

Rachel had never met Lucas's older brother. Would she ever see either of them if the war continued to go badly? She nibbled at something that looked like bacon but tasted like barbequed ribs. Perhaps war, not Prince Draven, would cause her death.

When Rachel finished eating, the footman led her upstairs.

"Sarah, announce Miss Rachel to Lord Baldwin," the footman said.

Moments later, she heard "Enter," and the door slid open.

Inside, three men in uniform sat across from Farold at a large wooden desk. They spoke and gestured at a map of space that floated in the air.

Rachel crept into the room, feeling out of place, but she remembered to curtsey and did so with a sway.

A large conference table stood to one side. Two men sat there, tapping on displays.

Farold stood. "Leave us, please. I need to speak privately with this lady."

Everyone marched toward the door except one man. "Sir, we need to—"

"Leave us. I'll deal with it shortly."

The man stood and left with the others.

Rachel stepped forward.

"Before Prince Draven arrives, I want to hear more about how you came to be with us." Farold gestured for her to sit.

"Okay." She sat across the desk from him. "Uh, where did I leave off? Oh, and how is Katherine?"

"Katherine is still bruised and sore, but she is awake and recovering. You may see her later today. The last thing you told me was how the Valac sang to you. Tell me more about that."

Rachel briefly described the Valac singing on the warship. "But they had more of a chance to sing after they attacked Katherine's ship. They cut two holes and entered."

He nodded. "I've inspected the breaches."

"I killed several Valac. They seemed like monsters on the planet, and later on the warship. But on Katherine's ship, when they surrounded me, they didn't hurt me. They sang. That's the only way I can describe it; they sang to me. I don't really understand the images that entered my mind, but I felt they didn't want to fight."

"They have a most unusual way of showing it."

Sarah appeared in the center of the room. "Prince Draven's dart has landed on the front lawn."

"Thank you, Sarah." Farold tapped on the display before him. "Ensure that no one on the staff resists his entry." He turned in his chair and gazed into the sky for several moments. Then in a barely audible whisper said, "I believe there is a spy in my household."

Rachel hoped he didn't think she was the spy.

"Sir?" Rachel spoke so softly she hardly heard herself. "Could you ask the prince to release Naomi? She's done nothing wrong."

"Yes. I shall," Farold said slowly. Then he returned his gaze to the window.

As the door opened and Prince Draven entered, Alton announced his arrival.

Lord Baldwin stood and bowed. "Welcome again to my home, Your Highness."

Rachel curtsied.

Prince Draven smiled. "You did say there was no need to knock."

"Indeed I did, and where you landed is so close and convenient to the front door. I'll just have the gardener replant the burn spots." Farold motioned toward the chairs. "Shall we sit and talk?"

The prince sat, followed by Farold. Rachel retreated to the conference table.

"There is little to talk about. I'm confident you can handle the hysterical ranting of your daughter." Prince Draven pointed to Rachel. "Hand over that provocateur, and I'll leave."

Rachel gripped her chair as bile rose in her throat.

Like stone, Farold's face remained unchanged. "Release my daughter's lady's maid, Naomi, and I'll forget this matter."

"What? The helot? Why are you concerned about her?"

"I'm concerned about everyone on my staff."

"How noble." Draven smirked. "She's under arrest for the murder of a Nightwatch operative."

"An operative who tried to kill my daughter." Farold took a deep breath. "May I speak frankly, Your Highness?"

Prince Draven waved his hand for Farold to continue.

"If you had arrested just this girl, Rachel, I never would've become involved. It was a clumsy attempt to silence all who know of Earth."

The prince's eyes flared wide.

"Yes, Sire, I know the truth. Your father likes his ale and talks all the more freely after enjoying several pints. As I was saying, your attempt to kill my daughter, and perhaps my sons, has involved me."

"I have taken no action against your sons."

The slightest hint of a grin appeared on Farold's face. He nodded. "But I am now involved and will remain so."

"This is a matter for Star Chamber."

"Yet you involved my loyal family."

"Your so-called loyal family became involved with the provocateur."

"We all know she's not a provocateur." Farold leaned back in his chair. "She has spoken truthfully of being from Earth and wants nothing more than to return home."

"That is treason enough. If you can guarantee the silence of Katherine and Lucas, I will leave them both out of this matter. "But," Draven pointed again to Rachel, "that one comes with me now. Knowledge of the existence of Earth is an infection. It will spread and eat at the fabric of our society. Therefore it must be eradicated."

Farold shook his head. "It is already leaking out, and nothing can stop it."

Draven's face flushed. "I am a prince and a high magistrate of Star Chamber."

"You are a prince, not the Prince Royal, but a prince, and you are one of five high magistrates of Star Chamber. However, I remain the marquis of this star system and the fleet admiral in this combat region. I am the supreme law of this system until the Valac are repulsed."

Draven's face paled. "So be it. But when the battle is won, I shall arrest her, and all who gave her aid her."

The prince stormed from the room.

Chapter 6

Prior system, Planet Delta

Lieutenant Tybalt Archer crossed the dart landing area through throngs of marines. Thousands of new men had just landed on the desert planet and formed into platoons and companies. They wore clean combat armor and carried pristine battle lances.

However, most, like him, would soon leave. Like Tybalt, these veterans of the Prior system battles wore armor clogged with grit and uniforms stained with sweat and both human and alien blood.

He didn't know where he'd fight next or exactly when, but the urgency with which the generals moved men and equipment told him the next fight would come soon.

As he crossed the pavement, Tybalt heard a familiar voice call his name and turned in that direction.

Chief Sadler saluted as he neared. "Captain Marin sent me to find you, sir."

"My suit's power pack is dead." Tybalt looked down at the slot. "I was going to get a new one."

"Don't bother. The *Argonaut*, along with your marine unit, has been ordered back to the Devon system." He pointed to a nearby hanger. "*Argonaut* darts are loading there. Report as soon as you've assembled your men."

Again they saluted, and the chief jogged away.

It wouldn't take long to assemble the unit; so many of his men had died on this orange rock. He tried not to think of his platoon in terms of death. *Be glad for those that lived and would soon return home.* Tybalt went to tell his men the news.

When Tybalt reported with the remnants of his platoon, Captain Marin invited him to fly up to the *Argonaut* with the other officers. Tybalt would've preferred to ride with his men, but such invitations were not refused.

"Thank you, sir." He saluted Captain Marin and boarded the officer's Espada-class dart.

By custom, the junior officers, like Tybalt, boarded first; the captain and other senior officers would board just before takeoff.

Tybalt sat next to a young ensign. He strapped in and turned to the new officer. "Hello, I'm Lieutenant Archer. Is this your first mission?"

"Yes. Is it that obvious? I'm Ensign Norris. I arrived yesterday from the academy."

"It's easy to spot the new guys." *They look terrified.* Tybalt shook the ensign's hand. "So you're twenty?"

"Yes, just." He frowned. "My birthday passed while coming here."

"Did you arrive during the combat?"

"No, after all the fighting, thankfully."

Tybalt grinned. *You're older than me or Lucas when we first fought the Valac.*

The senior officers boarded, followed by Captain Marin. When all were in and secure, the dart roared into the air.

As the craft reached space and gravity faded, Norris's face paled, and he leaned forward.

Tybalt hoped Norris wouldn't vomit.

Moments later, Norris sat up with the color restored to his face.

Memories of his first combat mission drifted through Tybalt's mind. At only sixteen, he'd left home to serve as a squire for Victor, Lucas's older brother. They'd attacked some unnamed airless moon. The first few days of fighting left him longing for sleep. Every sound or movement made him tense, and bile would lurch into his throat. He'd puked into his helmet more than once.

After nearly ten years of service, Tybalt was a combat veteran. The Valac no longer frightened him. Sleep did. How many men had died under his command? Their faces, their voices, and their screams haunted his dreams.

Tybalt shook his head, trying to clear his thoughts. Again, he turned to Norris. "So why did command send you to the Prior system, just to board a ship headed to the Devon system?"

"I'm studying to be a doctor, and the *Argonaut* is taking nearly a thousand wounded back to hospitals in that system."

"Oh." The faces of the wounded filled Tybalt's mind. "I'll have to see if anyone I know is on board."

The dart docked with the *Argonaut*, and sailors opened the hatch.

The boatswain whistle sounded, and the ship's bell rung. "*Argonaut* arriving," resounded over the vox system, and the boatswain whistled the captain aboard.

As soon as Tybalt cleared the quarterdeck, he hurried to his tiny office, aft of the marine operations center. There, he located a charged power pack and snapped it into his armor. The communications system engaged and logged into the ship's web.

Tybalt walked along the familiar passageway as he checked the manifest on his sleeve screen. Many seriously wounded were on board, but he looked for one in particular. As he entered the cargo bay, he came upon the entry, "Cornet Lucas Baldwin S438." The letter and numbers told Tybalt that he could find his friend in hypothermic stasis chamber 438.

Relieved that his friend was near, Tybalt walked along the line of chambers bolted to the deck, checked faces, and counted off numbers. He tried not to look at the injuries. Only the most grievous landed in stasis. Most had lost multiple limbs. Savage chest and gut wounds were also common. He'd seen such injuries before, but to see one after another tore at his soul.

The chambers stood side-by-side to conserve space. Most of the wounded hovered head-up in their coffin-like compartments, while others hung head down. Tybalt supposed it made no difference to the men in stasis, but he hoped to find Lucas upright.

Careful to step over all the tubes and wires that meandered along the floor and between the chambers, Tybalt continued his grim inspection until he reached

438. He nodded with relief. Lucas stood upright, as a man—a warrior—should.

Tybalt felt a pang of jealousy. Lucas's face displayed none of the agony of his last conscious moments, only the pleasant nothingness of peaceful sleep. Someday Tybalt hoped to regain such rest.

As the battle for Prior Four wrapped up, and the platoon had killed the last of the Valac, they had discovered Lucas in the cave. The medicus examined him and declared that Lucas would die without immediate treatment at a hospital. Tybalt barely had a moment to say goodbye before the dart rocketed into the sky with his friend.

Now Tybalt stepped back and stared at his sleeping friend. He needed to see all that Lucas had suffered.

Cuts and bruises crisscrossed Lucas's body. Some of the cuts were so deep they reminded Tybalt of floggings he had witnessed. No, he wouldn't think of his friend as being flogged. Bathed now in healing fluid, those wounds would become the scars that marked a hero's body.

But those cuts were minor in comparison to his limbs. Both arms were gone inches below the shoulder and one leg below the knee.

Tybalt saluted his unconscious friend and retraced his route out of the cargo bay. Months of painful recovery lay ahead for Lucas, but he was alive. They both were, and in three days they would arrive home on Exeter.

*   *   *

Devon system, Planet Exeter

Lord Admiral Farold Baldwin pushed open the door in the basement of Camden House. In his younger days he had used the stairs to go between the house and magrail station below. But these last few years, the hoist seemed more practical—or perhaps fifty feet just seemed longer. He entered the small compartment and pressed the button.

In moments, he arrived at the station where his magcoach waited to take him to the operations and command center beneath Camden Peak. That short journey would be enough time for him to ponder how all the recent events tied together. He sat alone at a table in a plush chair and organized his thoughts.

After more than a year of relative quiet, the Valac had staged a massive offensive across a wide front. Why?

Rachel wouldn't have figured in Farold's musings, but Prince Draven's actions puzzled him. Normally, Star Chamber would issue a warrant, and the unfortunate person would be arrested by local authorities and disappear, never to be seen or heard from again. Why attempt to kill Katherine, Rachel, and Naomi and make it look like a dart accident? Why involve Nightwatch?

His thoughts returned to Rachel. It seemed possible, perhaps probable, that she came from Earth. Prince Draven believed so. If she did, most who held authority wouldn't want that knowledge revealed. All power within the Kingdoms of Terra rested on the alliance between the Mage, Aux, and humans.

However, the Valac would remain their common enemy, and the planets of Terra were now home. Wouldn't noble and commoner alike defend their home worlds, such as Exeter?

Rachel had mentioned that the Valac sang to her. Katherine had confirmed it. That was the most troubling fact. Were they attempting to communicate?

The mag-coach pulled into the command center station. This intrigue would have to wait; there remained a war to fight. As the door slid open, and he stepped from the coach, Farold spotted his aide, Ensign Shaw, waiting on the platform. "Since I had a full night of sleep, I take it the war situation hasn't changed significantly."

"Yes, Admiral, the strategic and tactical situation is stable."

Farold grunted his approval and marched toward the blast doors.

"There were attacks in the Prior and Efford systems a few hours ago." Shaw hurried to catch up. "Also, sir, a holo message from Prince Draven arrived for you minutes ago."

Farold sighed and slowed his pace. So much of his time was spent dealing with that little …. He shook his head. Best just to hear what the prince had to say, and get it done with. "When is the morning briefing?"

"In twenty minutes, Admiral."

That should be enough time. He hurried toward his office.

Farold sat at his desk overlooking the command center and tapped a button. A small panel rose before him.

He pressed his hand to the panel.

The device scanned his eye.

A computare voice announced, "Confirmed. Lord Admiral Farold Baldwin. What are your orders?"

"Secure mode, and display message from Prince Draven."

The door to his office locked with a thud, and the window overlooking the command center darkened as black as deep space.

The image of the prince appeared in the center of the room. "Duty calls me to Novam Terram but, as a gesture of good faith, I have released the helot, Naomi. While I wish to repair any breech between us, I must do my duty. However, those duties can wait until after the Valac are repulsed."

The image faded.

Farold stared at the portrait of King Aelfric on the wall as he imagined a chessboard. His white pieces stood in their first two rows, except for a single pawn, Rachel. He had moved her into his household and safety—for now. That move that put him, and his family, in jeopardy.

However, black had made several moves. Prince Draven releasing Naomi and then leaving the planet were certainly two calculated plays, but to what end?

Ensign Shaw called over the computare. "Sir, the Valac have attacked Efford again, and I have an urgent encrypted message from Admiral Hawke."

Chapter 7

Devon system, Planet Exeter

Farold kept his office in secure mode for the communication with Admiral Hawke. As soon as the holoview image appeared, Farold noted the concern etched in Admiral Hawke's brow. "Arthur, it's good to see you. I've just heard about the attack on the Efford system. Do you have an update on the strategic situation?"

"Yes, Admiral. I do." Hawke gritted his teeth. "My battlegroup has orders to leave the Efford system in three days."

"Where are you being sent?"

"We're to rejoin the Pegasus fleet and reinforce units in the Phoenix system. I was told the mission is classified and not to share the information with anyone. But I can foresee the strategic consequences and had to ensure that you knew about these orders."

Farold nodded slowly, pondering the situation. If Arthur's battlegroup left Efford, only the seven ships of Farold's Orion fleet would remain to defend the system, an impossible task. But if Farold saved his seven ships by ordering them to withdraw from Efford and rejoin the main part of the Orion fleet in the Devon system then

Efford, his primary supply route, would fall to the Valac. "Who gave the orders?"

"Fleet Admiral O'Brian, but I don't think he wanted to. He seemed tense and hesitant. When I asked him what would happen to you and the rest of Orion Fleet, he just shouted for me to get my ships out. I think the order came from Naval Headquarters."

"If it had come from high command, I would've already heard about it."

"Then who issued the order?"

"Just obey them, Arthur." Farold didn't want his friend involved any deeper. He forced a smile to his face. "Thank you."

Both men nodded, and the image dissolved.

Farold leaned back in his chair. He had three days to come up with a plan, or the whole Devon system would fall.

*   *   *

Rachel tried not to stare at the large green and yellow bruises that still covered much of Katherine's face. At least the swelling around Katherine's eyes had decreased, allowing her to see again. "I don't mind helping you, if the doctor says it's okay."

Katherine smiled and turned her head toward Dr. Meredith.

The gray haired doctor nodded. "I think some time outdoors would be helpful." He returned to working with his palmcomp.

Rachel held her arm out to Katherine. "Then I'll help you go outside."

"We have servants for that." Katherine stumbled and clutched tight to Rachel as she rose from the bed.

"I'm your friend. I don't mind, but are your legs that weak?"

"That's due to the gravbed," Meredith said without looking up from the device in his hand.

Rachel didn't know the meaning of "gravbed" and cast him a confused glance.

Katherine shook her head.

Arms wrapped around each other's waists, they left the room and headed down the hall.

When they were alone, Katherine said, "I don't know how much Dr. Meredith knows about you being from Earth. The bed reduces the gravity around a patient."

"Oh." Rachel remembered feeling heavier when she got out of the hospital bed. "Oh. I get it now." Every time this world started feeling a little normal or comfortable, something strange dropped into her life.

Katherine clutched tight and leaned in to Rachel. "At least get Anna to help you."

"She's bringing us food in the garden." Rachel raised her arm, displaying her bracelet. At the top of the stairs they paused. "It still amazes me that you don't have an elevator … uh, lift, in this huge mansion."

"There's one for Father's use, and we have several, for everyone, in the city house."

"Fat lot of good they do us here. When you're ready we'll take the steps one at a time."

Still holding tight to Rachel, Katherine placed one foot on a step and then the other as she crept down to the first floor. "Has anyone seen Naomi?"

Rachel shook her head. "Your dad said Draven released her, but we don't know where she is yet."

Katherine grinned. "Earth must be such an informal place."

"What? Why do you think that?"

"You never seem to use titles."

Rachel thought for a moment. "Other than mister, doctor, and officer, I can't think of many I'd ever use."

"Those aren't even the ones I meant."

When they reached the foyer at the bottom of the stairs, Katherine sat on the couch where Rachel had sat just a day earlier. "I'm worried about Naomi. Few people ever return from Star Chamber."

Rachel sat next to her, thinking of the events just a day before. "Your father and Draven ... uh, *Prince* Draven ... stood face-to-face in this foyer just over a day ago and argued." She told Katherine all the events of that evening. "I thought I'd be arrested and taken to the Star Chamber place."

"Help me into the garden." Katherine stood. "Star Chamber is not so much a place as it is a court, a special one that acts when treason against the crown is suspected."

Using the bracelet, Rachel called for a footman who came and opened the massive front doors of the mansion.

"Shall I get someone to assist you, Daughter …?" His face flushed. "Uh, Miss Rachel?"

"No. We're fine. Thank you."

Treading with care, Rachel helped Katherine out the door.

When the door shut, Katherine looked at Rachel with pursed lips and wide eyes. "Knowledge that you may be the Daughter of Earth appears to be spreading."

"Well, Naomi told the other servants right after the crash, and you woke up briefly during your recovery and talked about it."

"I don't recall waking." Katherine continued down the front steps of the house with Rachel's help.

The lawn spread out for acres before them. Just to the right of the front door, a gardener tilled and replanted grass on four burn spots.

The two followed a gravel path to the left where flowers, bushes, and shade trees grew along a hillside.

Katherine pointed to seats at the edge of the garden. "Certainly, my careless words contributed to your dilemma and Naomi's arrest."

Rachel sat in a chair beside Katherine. "We'll find Naomi, and then everything will be okay."

But she didn't believe her own words. Either Prince Draven would have them killed, or the war would continue to go badly and they would die.

Often since she awoke on Lepeus Delta she had felt the need to pray, but could God even hear her on this distant world?

Please, God, if you can hear me, bring Naomi home. Keep Katherine and me safe, and bring me home to my family on Earth.

* * *

Farold sat behind his desk, leaning his head on his hand. He couldn't prove it, but he suspected that a widespread fear of Rachel lay behind all of the current intrigue. The easiest thing to do would be to turn her over to Star Chamber and beg the forgiveness of King Aelfric.

But Farold had known for years that Earth existed and done nothing with the knowledge. Brave men had fought and died to protect kingdoms built upon a lie, and he'd done nothing. Helots and others had lived as a subjugated people because they declared the truth, and he'd done nothing.

If he confronted the Privy Council with what he knew, they'd burn him at the stake. He needed evidence and a plan, but he had neither.

"Sir?" Shaw's voice said over the vox. "It's time for the morning briefing."

"Send in my senior staff. I have some news to share with them."

When the five sat across from him, Farold shared the strategic situation. "In three days, we need to be ready to hold the Efford system with the forces we have now, and thereby keep the supply line open. Or we must abandon Efford and make do with what we have."

"I know the Phoenix system has been attacked." One officer shook his head. "But there's nothing of strategic importance there. A small mining facility and a reconnaissance base, that's all. Its loss would have little impact. But if Efford falls, that would be catastrophic for millions."

"Let's not worry about Phoenix." Farold waved him quiet. "Worry about what we can change."

"We should evacuate as many women and children as possible from Devon to planets farther from the front, like Brittany and Essex," another stated.

"I agree." Farold nodded.

"We can mobilize cargo ships and space liners. Your yacht could hold several thousand."

"Load them full of refugees on the way out." Farold rubbed his chin. "And on the return trip, bring in needed supplies. But for morale's sake, my family will remain until the last refugee ship leaves."

Chapter 8

Devon system, Planet Exeter

Whenever Rachel tried to relax and clear her head, the notes of the Valac song filled the void. Still, she slumped in the chair, closed her eyes, and let the Devon sun warm her face. In moments, the notes resumed.

She opened her eyes and turned to Katherine. "Do you think the Valac will attack Exeter?"

Katherine stared at a nearby mountain. "My father is a better admiral than a parent."

"I'm glad to hear that, but he does love you."

"Yes." She nodded. "I know he does, but he rarely shows it."

Rachel gaped. "He gave you a spaceship."

Anna arrived, carrying two platters of food and drinks. Without a word, she set the items on the table between Rachel and Katherine.

"Thank you, Anna. That will be all." Katherine sipped her drink.

Anna curtsied and walked away.

Katherine nibbled on the meat and cheese until they were alone again. Then she spoke of her meeting with Prince Draven and Magnus, the Prince Royal, at a dance on Novam Terram. "Father thought it might be a good idea if I married one of them. While he tried to convince me, I asked for my own dart."

Rachel scrunched her face. "I don't know the Prince Royal guy, but I'd rather have died in the crash than marry Draven."

Katherine nodded. "I, too, would rather die than marry Prince Draven, and I'm certain Father no longer favors such a union. Prince Magnus is certainly the better choice, but he seems more interested in books, and my heart lies elsewhere."

"With Tybalt?" Rachel grinned and then sampled a drink of sweet and tangy fruits.

Katherine's eyes widened. "Did I say something while recovering?"

"No, but on your ship, when his holo image appeared, I saw the look in your eyes."

"I must hide my thoughts better." She shook her head. "Never say anything about this to my father. He would never allow it."

"Really?" Rachel frowned. "But why not? You love him, and he seems like a really nice guy."

"He is nice." Katherine smiled. "But Tybalt's father was a commoner until my father arranged for his elevation to baronet."

"Why is that important?"

"As the heir to the baronetcy, Tybalt is a member of the aristocracy, but not the nobility."

"Your family, the Baldwins, are nobles?"

"Yes." Katherine sipped her drink.

Rachel still didn't understand the details of social ranks, but some things were in better focus. Tybalt was nice and well-off. Katherine and the whole Baldwin family were nobles, and Rachel now lived in a weird world of war, romance, and intrigue.

The intrigue brought to mind the crystal Tybalt had given her. She mentioned it to Katherine. "I guess I lost it in the crash."

Katherine cast a sly smile and pulled it from the bodice of her dress. "It was in a pocket of my jumpsuit. I found it in a basket with my bracelet and other jewelry that survived." She stared at it for a moment. "You should have it. Doctors and servants are spending too much around me. I can't keep it safe."

Rachel tucked the crystal in her own bodice.

With only the slightest sound, a dart flew above the lawn and landed behind nearby trees.

"Is there a landing area over there?" Rachel pointed in the direction the dart had flown.

"Yes." Katherine nodded. "That's where Prince Draven should have landed."

"But I saw someone land on the roof."

"Only Father uses that pad. His dart is there now."

The two continued to talk as a small vehicle, only a bit longer than a golf cart, zipped along the path and disappeared behind the trees. Within seconds, the cart hurried back into view, going toward the house as the dart lifted back into the sky.

"Is that normal?" Rachel pointed to the dart and then the vehicle.

Katherine swallowed. "Quite. It's probably a delivery for someone in the house."

They continued to chat until the feet scurrying along the stone path sounded behind them. Rachel turned in her seat.

Anna burst into the clearing and hurriedly curtsied. "Naomi has been brought back to us—nearly dead."

* * *

Onboard the HMS Argonaut enroute to the Devon System

Technicians talked, and equipment hummed, chirped, and dinged, but Tybalt paid little attention. His mind focused on the strategic map projected by the holoview in the marine operations center.

As he stared, the Valac plan became clear. First they had attacked along a wide front, probably to spread the Terran forces thin. Most of the front had calmed except around Devon. There, the fight raged with the Valac now a hundred Gellers deep into Terran space.

Talons of Valac warships arced around Devon, ready to close and crush. But why would the Valac choose to destroy Devon?

For a moment, Tybalt wondered if it had anything to do with Rachel. He shook his head. Why would the Valac care about the Earth or someone from there?

It didn't really matter why. The Valac were concentrating around Devon. They were attacking, so it must be defended. Tybalt imagined hundreds of ships, many larger and more powerful than the *Argonaut*, racing to protect the Devon system. In less than two days Tybalt would arrive there with those other ships, ready to defend his home and family.

* * *

Devon system, Planet Exeter

Since discovering that Earth *did* exist and that early Terran history had been fabricated, Farold had struggled to be a just and fair lord of the helots within his territory. He had stopped the pogroms and prosecution of helots within the star systems he controlled. However, they remained a segregated minority serving in the most menial capacity—and groups of them made him nervous. He had his mother to thank for that.

Farold recalled his mother telling him numerous horrid stories or her saying, "Go out and play, but if you go too far into the woods alone, the helots will catch and eat you."

He could face a fleet of Valac warships, but a room full of helots made him retreat to the door.

Silently, he watched as most of the female staff, along with his wife, daughter, and Rachel clustered around Naomi's gravbed. A hundred years ago, during a prior Valac offensive, Farold's grandfather had converted this wing of the house into a hospital. It might be used that way again soon.

Anna hurried in carrying additional towels and bedding into the room.

"I told them everything." Naomi grabbed Rachel's arm. "I wanted them to stop hurting me, if just for a moment, so I told them everything … anything I could about the Earth still existing and that you're the Daughter of Earth. I even said that Prince Draven knew."

Several of the staff gasped.

"I'm sorry I was so weak." Naomi slumped onto the bed.

Farold's stomach turned as a tearful Naomi told of being beaten and her arms pulled from their sockets. He had forbidden his own security forces from routinely using torture, but he had no authority over Nightwatch.

Rachel leaned close. "You did nothing wrong. Just rest for now."

Farold gritted his teeth at Naomi's admission of treason. He had suspected the staff knew about Earth and of Rachel being called the Daughter of Earth; now he was certain.

Dr. Meredith approached him. "Both arms and several fingers were dislocated. I've reset them. She has old cuts and bruises from the crash and new bruises from being beaten. She also lost several more teeth, but she will live. I've given her medication for pain and to help her sleep."

Farold nodded. "Thank you, Doctor."

"What I heard her say the night of the crash and today is treason enough to have anyone executed." The doctor shook his head. "Why would Star Chamber release her?"

"I'm still trying to figure that out." Farold placed his hand on the door, and it slid open. "Return to your normal duties at the command center, Doctor."

Farold continued to stare at Naomi. They'd tortured her, but her injuries weren't life threatening as some had hysterically reported. He was thankful Prince Draven hadn't killed Naomi, but he wondered why. She was a helot and, as the doctor had said, admitted to treason. Most were killed within hours of such an admission, and no one would question such an execution—at least not out loud.

Prince Draven hadn't released Naomi out of mercy or as a gesture of good faith. Each action he took was a chess move and Naomi was just a pawn of the prince.

Chapter 9

Onboard the HMS Argonaut enroute to the Efford System

The jump alarm sounded, and the feeling of spinning and sliding swept through Tybalt. He grabbed the rail in front of him, and the sensation faded. He thought of Lucas and how he struggled to hide that space jumps made him sick. To Tybalt, it felt like being on a ride at a festival: weird and amusing at the time, and then over.

A thunderous boom shook the *Argonaut* the moment it returned to normal space. Tybalt stared at the holographic projection in the center of the room. A dozen Valac dreadnaughts raced toward the *Argonaut* and the seven other nearby Terran vessels.

The ship rattled again as a blast filled the screen.

"Incoming message from the Efford marine commander," a technician announced.

Tybalt pointed to the rear of the compartment. "Send his transmission to the office." He jogged toward the door.

As he entered, the center of the room brightened, the air seemed to shimmer, and the image of a young marine came into focus. "I'm Second Lieutenant Carson, senior surviving officer of the Efford detachment." Carson saluted Tybalt. "We've been waiting for you."

Only then did Tybalt realize that he must be the senior marine officer in the system. "Why were you waiting? What's the tactical situation?"

"The fleet is withdrawing from Efford. Admiral Baldwin orders that you jump immediately to Devon. The battlegroup will defend your rear and follow you."

"I'll make sure the captain is aware of the orders." Tybalt switched the holoview to the bridge. "Captain, did you receive orders to jump to Devon?"

"Yes. We're spinning the engines up now, but get your men ready for combat. The Valac are maneuvering to attack us again."

* * *

Devon system, Planet Exeter

Militarily, Farold knew it amounted to a suicide mission, but no one had ever surrendered to the Valac. If they couldn't win, they retreated, regrouped, and fought again. Retreat from the Devon system was not an option, and there were no units to regroup with, so he would fight to the last man.

"Admiral Baldwin?" Ensign Shaw stood at the door of his office.

Farold looked up from his palmcomp without a word.

"The last ship has left space dock. The fleet is ready to deploy."

"We'll break orbit immediately after the Last Night festivities." Farold leaned back in his chair and sighed.

"Ensure everyone here has a few hours with their families tonight. I'll fly to the opening ceremony with mine."

"Yes, Admiral."

Farold had hoped more people would be evacuated before the Efford jump point fell. He'd hoped his own family would leave, but his wife, Charlotte, had refused. They'd evacuated over 180,000 women and children, but that only amounted to a tiny fraction of the population.

In moments, the last Terran vessels would jump away from Efford, and the Valac would control all the supply routes.

King Aelfric had abandoned him. Why? Because Rachel was from Earth, and Farold knew it? Did that knowledge so endanger the power of the nobles and peers? Were the Kingdoms of Terra so wrought with fear?

Farold had to conclude that they were, that their power—his power—rested on the myth that the Valac had destroyed Earth, and that humans now aided the Mage in a fight against a common enemy.

If the Valac were attempting to communicate through Rachel, that might explain some of the recent treachery from those in power in the kingdom. This endless war served to solidify their power. Such power brokers would need to destroy any hint of dialogue with the Valac. What if the Valac did want peace? Without a war, would there be an alliance? Would those in power be able to hold on to it?

He had questions, suppositions, but few facts.

Still, Prince Draven had given him the option to turn Rachel over, and he'd refused.

He slammed his fist on the desk and laughed bitterly. In trying to save Rachel, he had ensured his own death and that of his family. Indeed, he'd signed the death warrant for the entire Devon system.

*   *   *

Each morning, Rachel awoke to the fading sounds of the Valac song. Staying busy seemed to keep the notes at bay and free her mind of the notion that she might be going crazy, so she tended to Naomi.

Katherine insisted that the servants could handle Naomi's recovery, but Rachel wouldn't delegate the care. Beyond keeping her mind occupied, she felt responsible for every bruise and cut that Naomi had suffered.

Despite spending most hours nursing Naomi, Rachel had sensed a rise in tension. Soldiers, many about her age, hurried through the mansion. Darts landed on the pad out front and, when it was occupied, on the lawn. The old gardener had given up fixing burn spots.

While in the gardens, Katherine had pointed out Camden Peak, the snow-covered mountain that crowned the fleet command center. Later, Rachel watched as dozens of darts shot into the sky from camouflaged tunnels within the mountain.

Occupied with Naomi's care, Rachel rarely saw anyone other than Katherine and Anna. She assumed Farold spent his days planning attacks and counterattacks as the front grew ever closer to Devon. Katherine mentioned that her mother had converted the north wing of the mansion into a hospital.

Rachel talked with Naomi, still lying in bed, when the holographic image of Sarah appeared in the room. "Lady Katherine wishes to speak with you." The image shimmered, and Katherine appeared.

Naomi attempted to stand, but Rachel stopped her.

"There's a huge event in the city tonight. It's called Last Night, and Mother wants us to attend."

"Us? Me?" Rachel slapped her hand to her chest. "Do I have to go?"

Naomi giggled.

Katherine glared at her and then turned to Rachel with a softer look. "When Mother decides everyone should go to something, even Father can rarely avoid attending. I think we'll all be there."

Rachel stepped closer to the projection. "What kind of event is this?"

"It's a ceremony, concert, ball, party, and …" Katherine paused and her whole body seemed to droop. "Well, the entire fleet deploys tonight in defense of Devon. It's the sendoff of our sailors and marines into battle."

"Oh." Rachel stood. "Your father's going? Are you sure you're up to this thing?"

"As the daughter of the Lord and Admiral, I am expected."

"I see." Rachel didn't know whether to display a sympathetic grin or sadness, so she remained stoic. "Of course I'll go with you. When do we leave?"

"In an hour."

After a momentary glimmer, the image disappeared.

Rachel sat by Naomi's bedside, wondering if this might be the beginning of the end.

Slowly, and with a few grimaces, Naomi sat up. "Anna told me that she asked you to save me from Star Chamber."

Rachel nodded. "I did what I could."

"Katherine is kinder than she sometimes appears, more so since the crash, but her father has always been a thoughtful and just man. Save him, please."

"I'm just a girl from Earth." Rachel squeezed her hand. "I've got to get Anna in here to look after you, and I'm sure she'll want to dress me like a Victorian fashion model."

An hour later, on the roof of the mansion, Rachel stood in a lace gown that gradually changed from midnight blue to azure, and every shade between. Even the polish on her nails changed color to match.

While there, she admired the view of nearby forests and lawns and wondered if she was in the right place. A dart sat nearby, but it seemed empty.

Then a man in a black jumpsuit hurried out the nearby roof door, nodded to Rachel, and continued to the dart.

Now convinced she was in the right place, she returned her gaze to the view.

Seconds later, Farold, in a pristine uniform of navy blue and gold, strode from the mansion.

Rachel curtsied awkwardly.

Jumpsuit man came to the hatch and saluted. "Good evening, Admiral."

Farold returned his salute. "When we arrive at the coliseum, remain with the dart. I'll be leaving immediately after the ceremony."

Several minutes later, Lady Baldwin strolled from the mansion, followed by Katherine and two uniformed bodyguards.

Katherine smiled as she strolled by, but said nothing. No bruises were visible on her face and arms. Rachel followed her up the ramp.

When she stepped inside, Rachel almost imagined that she stood in a plush, private train car. Deep rust-orange carpet, polished wood walls, gold-framed lights, and black leather seats all conveyed wealth.

Katherine gestured for Rachel to sit facing her in seats near the rear while her parents sat in front.

"How did you get the bruises to disappear?" Rachel asked.

"A generous use of makeup." Katherine grinned.

Rachel glanced out the elongated window between them as the dart lifted into the air. "Where's the ceremony being held?"

"In the capital city, New Plymouth. We'll be there in just a few minutes."

Katherine showed little inclination to talk, so Rachel enjoyed the view out the window. The sun hung low in the sky, but enough light remained to see mountains, rivers, forests, and the towers of a city on both sides of a large river.

The yellow rays of the Devon sun created illusions of golden spires with cylindrical, rectangular, and pyramid-like steel towers that rose high into the sky. Narrow, train-like vehicles shot along monorail lines through the city and across the wide river while thousands of darts coursed through the sky on roads of air.

Rachel turned from the window. "I had no idea so many people lived on this world."

"About ten million in the capital."

Rachel returned her gaze to the city. Much of the ground seemed parklike, with many roads and monorails high above the green grass and trees. As the dart turned, a domed coliseum rose into view.

"Is that where we're going?"

Katherine nodded.

Within seconds, they landed on a building beside the stadium.

Stepping from the dart, Rachel twisted about as she attempted to take in the strange city surrounding her. Vid images announced the latest news from giant screens on nearby towers. People ambled to the stadium on glass and steel walkways suspended between buildings.

Katherine took her hand. "We need to go."

On a walkway high in the air, they crossed to the stadium, and stepped onto a lift that lowered them to the main ring of seats. From there, they strolled to a booth that could have held twenty, but only Farold, Charlotte, Katherine, and Rachel entered. The two bodyguards remained just outside the door.

When everyone took their seats, giant displays around the stadium showed happy scenes from the crowd. Then it shifted to men standing along the edge of the field behind kettledrums and others with long trumpet-like horns at their side. A single man in uniform marched to the center of the field.

Rachel gasped as the image on the screen changed to her and Katherine. Rachel closed her mouth and tried not to look startled.

As the view slid to Farold, he stood and announced, "Tomorrow, the entire Orion Fleet sails in defense of Devon. Let the Last Night festivities begin."

His words reverberated through the coliseum.

Katherine and her mother stood, and Rachel followed as the crowd rose with a roar.

Drummers thundered out a beat, and trumpets blared.

Then silence reigned.

The voice of the lone man at the center of the field rose in acapella song.

> *"God of Earth we pray You keep,*
> *Those brave men who sail the deep.*
> *They climb the heavens to save,*
> *The remnant loyal, few and brave,*
> *And so they trust in Your might,*
> *Be with them through the night.*
> *With You, they are the point of the Sword,*
> *And victory is their only reward."*

Everyone in the booth remained standing, watching the singer as he continued, but Rachel fixed her gaze on a bodyguard speaking with Farold. Together, they stepped to the rear of the booth.

Rachel blinked in disbelief. Tybalt had arrived from somewhere. Their eyes met and she smiled.

Tybalt nodded at her and then saluted Farold. The two men spoke, but Rachel couldn't hear the words.

Katherine looked to Rachel and then followed her gaze. She jumped to her feet and ran to the men. An animated discussion commenced. After several moments, Farold placed a hand on Katherine's shoulder and they walked back to their seats. Tybalt followed but sat several rows back.

Farold wrapped his arm around his daughter as they sat, but Katherine seemed near tears.

Rachel squeezed her hand. "I'm sure your father and Tybalt will be fine."

With a nod, Katherine leaned close and whispered, "Lucas is here, but he's been badly wounded."

Chapter 10

Devon system, Planet Exeter

"Badly wounded?" Rachel tensed. "What does that mean exactly?"

"I don't know." Katherine frowned. "Tybalt sent the report to father's palmcomp, but he won't read it until Last Night festivities are over, and he ordered Tybalt not to tell me or anyone else."

Rachel looked down the row at Farold. He stared straight ahead. *How can he watch this knowing his wounded son is at home? Does his wife, Charlotte know? How could she be calm?*

Katherine huffed. "Men."

"Some things are universal." Rachel nodded. For the rest of the concert, her thoughts centered not on the music, but on the injuries that Lucas may have suffered.

As the musicians and singers marched from the field, Rachel sighed and squeezed Katherine's hand. "You'll be home soon."

Katherine shook her head and hurried on.

Tybalt strolled across the skyway with Rachel, but they didn't board the dart. Instead, Farold led them into the building and into a lift.

When the doors of the compartment closed and the descent began, Farold sighed. "This is one of my least enjoyable duties."

Charlotte gripped his hand. "The news conference?"

Farold nodded. "I'm a soldier, not an actor, but I always feel like I'm putting on a show at these events."

The doors opened to what looked like a television studio, and a dozen reporters, cameramen and others, all in military uniform, stood to attention.

Katherine, her mother, and Tybalt stopped at the rear of the studio. Rachel hid behind them, gazing at the room. She nudged Tybalt and whispered, "Is every man on the planet in the military?"

He nodded. "Except for young boys and old men, yes, but usually most aren't on active duty."

"Be seated." Farold moved to the lectern. "I understand you have a few questions for me."

"Admiral, how is the morale of the men? Are they ready for the next attack?"

"Morale has never been better. Every sailor, soldier, and marine in the Devon system is ready to take the battle to the Valac."

"Do you have everything you need to win, Admiral?"

"Has there ever been a commander who has gone into a fight saying they had too many warships, lances, or missiles? I want more of everything, but we will win with what we have."

Such questions continued for several minutes, and then a young, dark-haired marine journalist shouted, "Refugee ships stopped leaving a few hours ago, Admiral."

The room fell silent.

The journalist continued. "They had been evacuating large numbers of women and children. Has Efford fallen?"

Farold stared at the reporter for a moment. "The fleet withdrew from Efford in order to concentrate our forces in Devon."

Before Farold could point to someone else, the young journalist spoke again.

"But Admiral, if the Valac control Efford, resupply and reinforcement will be difficult. How can what remains of the Orion fleet be victorious over a larger Valac fleet?"

A flash of anger crossed Farold's face. "We don't know how many Valac ships will attack, but whenever and with whatever they do, the brave sailors of the Orion fleet, marine units, and planetary defense forces can and will achieve victory." A grin spread over Farold's face and he pointed to the marine journalist. "And you will be there to witness and document it all from my command ship."

The young man paled. "Thank you, Admiral, but—"

"I'll speak with you later. Perhaps we should let others ask a few questions." Farold pointed to another reporter.

After a dozen mostly easy questions, he held up his hand.

"Thank you all for your queries, but I have more Last Night events to attend before the fleet departs." Farold smiled and hurried from the platform as he talked with one of the guards.

The Camden entourage followed. Katherine stood by her mother, leaving Rachel and Tybalt in the rear with one of the guards.

Onboard the dart, Katherine glared at Tybalt.

He leaned close and whispered. "Your father would rather have you angry tonight than showing tears. Lucas will live."

Katherine huffed again, but gradually her face softened. "It's good to see you."

"It's good to be home again."

The dart flew above the city a large oval tower and landed on the roof. The entourage descended in the lift to a formal dance. After Lord and Lady Baldwin were announced to the hundreds in attendance, Katherine strolled about with her parents, smiling, talking, and shaking hands.

Walking over to a wall, Rachel tried to fade into it, but Tybalt joined her.

"Have you been assigned to watch me?"

"Watch over you, yes." He grinned. "Commoner friends of the family don't normally receive guards, but Lord Baldwin thought you might need someone."

Rachel chuckled. "I've been calling him Farold and his wife Charlotte."

Tybalt frowned. "You've learned Lingua Terra well. Perhaps now you should learn the customs and titles of Europa and the other Kingdoms of Terra."

"I will, and I'll be fine tonight. Go find a pretty girl and dance."

"I enjoy dances with friends, but not this. The formality, the old music, the coming battle …." He shook his head as he looked about.

Katherine stood only ten feet away, talking to a handsome, tanned marine.

Rachel decided to play matchmaker. She tilted her head in Katherine's direction. "You have a friend here."

"Yes, you're right." Tybalt held out his hand. "May I have this dance?"

"What? Ah … I."

He raised an eyebrow.

"I don't know this dance." *Actually, I don't know any of them.*

"Just follow my lead." He grinned.

Together they walked onto the dance floor as music swept through the room.

Tybalt stopped and smiled at Rachel.

She faced him, still wondering what to do.

He stepped close and with his left hand held her right. "See how the other women hold their partners? Do the same." He wrapped his right hand around her and placed it on her back. "I'll step forward. You step back."

Rachel stumbled, but she gradually learned the flow of movements.

As the music rose to a crescendo, Tybalt leaned close and whispered, "Do you have the crystal from the lunch bag?"

She glanced at her bodice. Tybalt had originally placed it in a lunch bag when they smuggled her off the *Argonaut.* She nodded, and they danced on.

As they whirled around the floor, a naval officer entered, and wove between the dancers to Farold.

"Look to your right. That officer just came in to talk to Fa … Lord Baldwin."

Tybalt shrugged. "Someone's always talking to him."

While Rachel spun and turned, she continued to watch as Farold and the officer conferred. Then the officer saluted and quickly exited the ballroom. Farold and Charlotte strolled about the room smiling, talking, and shaking hands, but always they moved closer to the door.

With a quick wave and nod, a guard signaled for Tybalt and Rachel to join them, and the entourage departed for the roof.

Despite her earlier misgivings Rachel had enjoyed the dance with Tybalt and wanted to continue. "Where are we going now?"

"To another dance." Katherine stepped out.

"Another one?" Rachel grinned as she followed. "How many are there?"

Katherine squinted at her father. "Five or six?"

"We're leaving for home." Farold stepped aside and let the ladies board the dart first.

"Well, at least we can see Lucas." Katherine scowled at her father.

"What?" Charlotte looked from Katherine to Farold. "Lucas is home?" She turned to Tybalt. "Did you bring the message?"

"I told Tybalt to remain silent." Farold held the hatch open. "Lucas is wounded but will live."

"Wounded?" Charlotte's eyes flared wide.

Katherine stared at her father. "Badly wounded from what I heard."

"My son hovers between life and death, and you don't tell me?" Her face flushed deeper red with each word.

"Calm yourself," Farold said.

"What?" Charlotte's glared at Farold. "My son is badly wounded and you tell me to calm myself?"

"The worst appears behind him." Farold sighed. "The sooner we all board the sooner we get home and see him."

Charlotte hurried onto the craft, and silence reigned on the trip back to Camden.

When the dart hatch opened, Charlotte and Katherine hurried out. Farold followed at a slower pace.

Tybalt held Rachel back. "They'll go to Lucas. We'll wait in the hall."

Despite being anxious to see Lucas, she nodded and lingered behind. As they left, Anna stood at the bottom of the ramp. She curtsied and led them to the appropriate room. Just outside the door, Anna joined Naomi and a few other servants while Rachel and Tybalt paced nearby.

After only a few minutes, the door opened, and Farold, with a face that showed no emotion, stepped into the hall. Alton followed him in a marine uniform. "I must leave. Lieutenant Archer, Sergeant Alton, accompany me. The rest of you return to your duties."

A moment later, Rachel leaned against the wall, and slid to the floor, as she wondered what to do.

Chapter 11

Devon system, Planet Exeter

Consumed by thoughts of the coming battle, Farold stepped from the mag-coach. Ensign Shaw stood nearby with palmcomp in-hand. "Admiral, all ships, including the *Veritas* and your other privateers, report full magazines and fuel loads. However—"

"Not now." Farold waved Shaw off. He strode across the platform beneath the fleet operations center. "Assemble the senior staff for a meeting in ten minutes."

"Yes, Admiral."

As Shaw hurried away, Farold told Sergeant Alton to head to the command ship *Rubicon*. "I'll see you there shortly."

Now alone with Tybalt, Farold said, "Follow me to my office."

When they arrived, he put the room in secure mode and detailed his suspicions.

Tybalt shook his head. "Prince Draven tried to kill Rachel, Katherine, and her maid? Does he have any evidence of treason or that Rachel is a provocateur?"

"Evidence? No, other than Rachel's claim that she's from Earth, though that's probably enough for Star Chamber to act." Farold took a deep breath. "But they survived the assassination attempt, and I blocked subsequent arrests. I believe that's why Devon and the Orion Fleet are surrounded and without reinforcements."

Tybalt shook his head. "I've been wrong about so much. I always thought you were …"

"What? That I was a loyal subject of the king?" Farold grinned. "I was. I *am*, but I knew more than I let on. I knew that Earth still existed somewhere out there in the void and that King Aelfric's power flowed from the lies of the Mage."

"And the king would sacrifice an entire planet to maintain that power?" Tybalt's face paled. "I shouldn't have tried to help Rachel or solve the mystery of her origins."

"You and my son sought the truth. There is no wrong in that." Farold placed his hand on Tybalt's shoulder. "Unfortunately, we've frightened the powers of the kingdom."

Tybalt rubbed his chin. "I apologize nonetheless."

"I've told you all of this because I know you're a loyal friend."

"I am loyal to you, Admiral, but the king's plot is huge. How do you know who to trust?"

Farold thought of his oldest son, Victor, still on duty with the Pegasus Fleet. "If you had been kept away from this trap, I wouldn't trust you, but you were sent into it. The king wants us all to die together."

Tybalt frowned. "I'm not afraid of death. If needed, I'll stand at your side, Admiral."

Farold gripped his arm and smiled. "You won't be at my side. I need you for a very special mission."

"Whatever you order, Admiral, I'll do it."

"Don't rush your answer." Farold sat on a nearby chair and gestured for Tybalt to sit. "Only part of this is an order. You are to remain here with your marines. Officially, you're here to guard the Camden Operations Center. That is the order. But please stay close to my family. If I fail to turn back the Valac, defend them and … well, I don't want them to suffer."

"What?" Tybalt shook his head. "I couldn't do that."

Memories of the Valac ripping limbs from marines, slicing them open and … Farold forced the thoughts from his mind. "You may find the strength if the Valac are victorious."

Farold unlocked the door, and the two parted in opposite directions.

He entered the nearby conference room and examined the faces of his senior staff—all experienced and intelligent men. They'd all read the current reports. They knew the state of affairs, and every one of them now wore a somber face.

There really was nothing to do but proceed as best they could.

"What is the latest intelligence?" Farold asked.

Commander Williams enlarged a section of the holo display in the center of the table. "Admiral, information from the stealth probe in the Efford system indicates the Valac have begun forming into battlegroups. The angle of these formations indicates a jump to the Devon system. However, their formations are incomplete, and they have not yet launched wasps, so we expect the attack to come no sooner than about five hours from now."

"Send the recall notice over all the vids." Farold leaned forward. "Our goal must be victory. Without it, we and our families will not survive. We are the point of the sword."

One hour later, the dart hatch opened and Farold marched across the quarterdeck of his command ship, *Rubicon*.

The boatswain blew his whistle, and the ship's bell rung. "Orion Fleet arriving," boomed over the vox system.

"What are your orders, Admiral?" Ensign Shaw asked.

"Deploy the fleet." Farold continued to the command center as the eighty-two ships of the Orion Fleet pulled out of Exeter orbit and, as planned, traveled deep into the shadow of the planet. When in position, the ships reduced power levels and heat venting to a minimum.

Such measures wouldn't hide them for long but, Farold hoped, it would give them the advantage of surprise.

*　*　*

Lucas's eyes fluttered open. He retched and struggled both to breathe and focus his vision. A man in white stood over him. *God?*

"I'm clearing your lungs of hypothermic fluid. Hold still."

Not God. But Lucas still endeavored to obey. He gagged again and struggled to remain calm.

Seconds later, the doctor rolled Lucas on his side. "Cough and breathe."

In this new position, Lucas noticed that his mother and sister stood on the far side of the room, and biobands covered the ends of stumps just inches below his shoulders.

He had no arms.

Lucas gasped and heaved again. After several more moments of coughing, gagging and wheezing, his breathing returned to normal. The doctor released him, and Lucas flopped onto his back.

Tilting his head, Lucas examined the room. Beeping and humming equipment beside the gravbed measured his brain activity, heart rate, blood pressure, oxygen level, and more. From the device, tubes flowed into what remained of both of his arms.

The doctor glanced at a display and made notes on his palmcomp.

Lucas held up the two stumps. "They both hurt a bit, and itch a lot. How badly was I injured?"

Katherine hurried to him. "Bad, but—"

"You'll make a full recovery," his mother added as she strode to his bedside.

Lucas looked at the doctor.

"You'll be fine." He slid his palmcomp into a pocket. "We'll start your recovery program tomorrow. I'll give you some time with your family." He left the room.

"What else happened?" Lucas stared at his chest. Several biobands covered large areas.

"Well, in addition to your arms, you still have lots of cuts and bruises, a few broken ribs— and one leg is gone." Katherine tapped just above his missing leg.

Lucas sighed as the facts stirred in his mind. He recalled his last conscious moments in the cave. "I didn't think I'd live." He grinned. "I'm glad to be … am I home?"

"Yes." His mother beamed. "You're at Camden House."

"Good." For several moments, Lucas breathed deeply. "How's the war going?"

"Not well. Efford fell yesterday. The Orion Fleet is regrouping in the Devon system." Katherine continued with what amounted to a classified briefing. "Father expects an attack on Devon and Exeter very soon."

"Then I need to get temporary arms and a leg. Sarah, I need you."

"Don't be in a rush." His mother brushed the stubble on his cheek. "You still have broken ribs and nasty cuts. A long recovery is ahead."

"I don't have the time. I refuse to die on my back."

Light shimmered, and Sarah appeared in the middle of the room. "Welcome home, Sir Lucas. How may I—"

"Get the doctor … what was his name?"

"Dr. Meredith," Katherine responded.

"Get Doctor Meredith back in here. I need … oh, what are they called … prosthesis. Several actually."

Sarah disappeared.

Lucas frowned. "So I escaped one battle only to find myself on the eve of another."

"I guess so, brother."

"Is our new friend safe?"

"Rachel?"

"That woman is *not* our friend." Mother huffed. "Rachel may get us all killed. I'll go find the doctor."

Katherine scowled as her mother left the room, and then turned back to Lucas. "For the moment, Rachel is well. She's probably nearby. Do you want me to get her?"

Lucas smiled and nodded.

*   *   *

Rachel moved several yards from the door after Lady Charlotte marched from the room with an angry glare. Then the door whooshed again, and a smiling Katherine stepped into the hallway.

"Lucas would like to see you."

"I don't know if I can go in there." Rachel stared at the door. "How seriously is he hurt?"

"Very badly." She described his injuries.

Tears welled in Rachel's eyes. "You can help him, right? You must have prosthetics. Probably really good ones."

"Yes. Most amputees use them. I'm sure Lucas will for a few months during his recovery."

"During his recovery? Why not after?"

"After?" Katherine's eyes narrowed. "Why would he need them after his limbs grow back?"

Chapter 12

Orion Fleet on Station in the Devon System

Farold hated waiting. In the past, his ships had coordinated with other fleets and battlegroups to stay on the offensive. He struggled to keep his face stoic, but sitting and waiting to be attacked churned his gut.

Naval command had denied every request for fleet support and most applications for munitions and supplies, citing higher priority needs, but Farold knew the real reason. King Aelfric feared the truth about Earth and would do whatever must be done to suppress it.

A hundred and twenty years ago, the need to quash all knowledge of Earth had led to the War of the Kingdoms, and the suppression of the losers as helots. Today, the king only needed the deaths of Farold, his family, servants, and Rachel, but to wipe all knowledge of Earth from existence, the king appeared ready to let Exeter and all her people perish as well.

Then only the lie would remain.

Were the Mage puppet masters? Did they require this mass murder, or were King Aelfric and his loyalists cold killers? Anger surged like fire within Farold.

Alarms sounded.

He would uncover the whole truth and find a way to destroy King Aelfric.

"Admiral, tunnels are forming," a technician announced.

Farold turned to the journalist who had asked him the tough questions earlier in the evening. "Start recording the story." He grinned at the young man. "If you live, you'll tell your grandchildren about this day."

The young man paled and switched on the vid recorder.

"Admiral, we've detected Valac warships emerging."

"Sound action stations."

*   *   *

Devon system, Planet Exeter

Rachel stepped into the room shaking her head. "Arms and legs don't grow back."

"I sure hope they still do," Lucas said from the gravbed.

"Of course they do," Katherine responded with a confused expression.

"Since when?" Rachel asked.

"Since always," Lucas struggled to sit up.

"No." Rachel still kept her distance. "Not for humans."

Katherine's eyes flared wide.

"Well, at least not for humans from Earth. Nothing grows back."

"Nothing?" Katherine shook her head. "You mean if your finger gets cut off it won't grow back?"

"That's right. It just stays a stump like ...." Rachel looked at Lucas as her words faded.

Lucas smiled. "Well, I'm glad these will grow back."

Katherine gazed at Rachel concern in her eyes. "Knowing that if you lost a finger, toe, arm, or whatever, that it would be gone forever—that would be scary."

The door slid open and Dr. Meredith walked in holding what looked like a black suitcase.

Worried that Dr. Meredith might not know of her Earth origins, Rachel stilled her tongue, but confusion raged within her.

* * *

Lucas squirmed on the bed, eager to be mobile again. Katherine and Rachel sat him on the edge of the bed. "How long will this take?"

Dr. Meredith held up a shiny steel arm from the case. "About an hour for the devices to connect with the proper nerves and to tune it to your brain." He clicked a steel band around the stump of Lucas's right arm. "Of course, it will take additional time to learn to use them."

With Katherine holding one shoulder, Rachel the other, Lucas sat watching the doctor as he made adjustments to both the length and width of the prosthetic.

"That should do it." Meredith tapped the band.

Lucas gritted his teeth as dozens of needles shot into his arm.

"This might hurt a bit." Meredith clicked the second one in place.

"Thanks for the warning." Needles shot into his left arm next.

"I would have preferred you wait until you had fully recovered from your broken bones and flesh wounds, but I commend your willingness to fight." Dr. Meredith clamped a ring around Lucas's leg stump. "Your father and brother will be proud."

Lucas frowned at the comparison to Victor. He grimaced as more needles pierced his leg.

Dr. Meredith continued fitting prosthetic limbs onto the bands of each stump, and then asked Lucas to perform certain movements.

Almost an hour later, Lucas stood, and stumbled forward.

Rachel caught and steadied him.

Light shimmered, and Sarah appeared in the middle of the room. "Excuse me, Lady Katherine. Lady Charlotte requests your assistance at the armory."

Lucas smiled gently. "Mother is probably frightened and wants a hand lance."

"Why?" Katherine shook her head. "She can't hit anything."

Still in Rachel's arms, he said, "Go and help her. The doctor and Rachel will assist me."

An amused grin spread across Katherine's face. She turned and walked from the room.

With Rachel close beside him, Lucas continued around the room with a somewhat mechanical gait. He stopped and flexed his prosthetic fingers.

Meredith pulled a card from his pocket and set it on the table. "Try to pick it up."

Lucas struggled for nearly a minute, but finally held it up, and smiled.

"I'll get ready for incoming wounded," Dr. Meredith said. "You should be fine, but take it easy for now, and call if you need anything."

When they were alone, Lucas smiled and held out his new hand to Rachel. "I'm glad you're well."

Her face glowed as she clutched his prosthetic fingers. "I'm glad you will be."

Lucas wanted to spend time alone, getting to know Rachel, but he knew this was neither the time nor the place. "Perhaps we should find Mother and Katherine and get ready for what may come."

"Oh, yes. Why did your mother need Katherine to get a hand lance?"

"It takes two family members to open the armory door. Let's go find them and show off my new limbs."

"Temporary limbs." Rachel shook her head. "They'll really grow back? That's so weird. How and when did it start for Terrans?"

Lucas shrugged and smiled. "One more mystery to sort out—later. Sarah, where are Mother and Katherine?"

Light shimmered once more, and Sarah appeared in the middle of the room. "They remain in the armory with Alton."

"Alton? That's strange. He should be with Father on the *Rubicon*."

Rachel clutched his arm. "I don't know where the armory is, but I'll help you get there."

Lucas nodded. Together they exited the room, and hobbled down the hall.

"Did Katherine get you back here without incident?"

"No." Rachel shook her head. "We encountered Prince Draven on the Exeter skylift, and he ordered members of Nightwatch to kill us."

"*What?*" Anger boiled in Lucas as she detailed the crime. "I knew Prince Draven was a rogue, but not a murderer."

"There's more." Rachel held his arm tight as they descended the stairs. "When Draven discovered we were alive, he raided this house and demanded your father give me up, but he wouldn't."

Lucas concentrated as he took each step down several flights of stairs. His amputated limb hurt with each wobbly step to the basement. As they went Rachel continued to tell all that Lucas had missed.

Lucas squeezed Rachel's hand. "My father's efforts on your behalf please me greatly." His face warmed. He wanted to say more, but simply pointed down the hall. "It's this way."

A bang thundered along the passage, followed by a woman's scream.

Charging, stumbling, and weaving, Lucas hurried toward the armory and fell against the doorframe.

Just inside, Alton waved a hand lance and cursed.

"Alton? What's going on?" Lucas stepped into the opening.

Only then did he notice his mother on the floor with blood pooled around her.

"What happened?"

"He shot Mother!" Katherine leapt behind a counter. Alton swung around and fired on Lucas.

*   *   *

Orion Fleet on Station in the Devon System

The Orion Fleet hid in the shadow of their home planet, but the enemy didn't bother with stealth. Using just passive detectors, Farold watched as the Valac fleet thrust deeper into the Devon system.

The straightforward attack plan of the Valac didn't surprise Farold. It pleased him. With superior numbers, more than twice Farold's eighty ships, the Valac commander wasn't challenged to think in new and unusual ways.

Farold's attack would be unusual. He imagined the Valac commander's search for the human fleet. *Be patient and you'll find us.*

Most of the technicians in the operations center stared at their consoles. The few who looked at Farold appeared frightened and younger than he recalled. The journalist stood to one side of the compartment recording everything. Farold needed to ease the tension. "Where is Sergeant Alton? I need a cup of tea."

"He missed boarding, Admiral." The officer of the deck frowned.

The penalty for missing deployment was severe. For nearly twenty years, and through many battles, Alton had always been at his side, ready to serve. What could have kept him away this day?

Unwilling to show his concern to the crew, Farold grinned. "Well, someone get me that tea."

Within seconds, the desired cup arrived, and for several minutes Farold sipped at the drink, maintaining a relaxed appearance as the Valac flew ever closer.

"Admiral." A technician turned to Farold. "Valac detectors are sweeping our position."

Farold set the cup down on the console. "Execute the battle plan."

The navigation officer turned to the ethercomm tech. "Use evasive maneuvers option alpha."

"Spin up the engines to full," the engineering officer ordered. "Form a Mage Tunnel."

The jump alarm sounded as the Valac launched missiles.

Chapter 13

Orion Fleet on Station in the Devon System

"Jump," Farold commanded with a calm voice.

The Orion fleet raced across the event horizons of their Mage Tunnels with less than three hundred thousand miles remaining between them and the opposing Valac fleet. The enemy missiles raced ahead of the fleet, but found no targets.

Because of the proximity of the two fleets, the Orion ships emerged almost instantaneously less than two hundred miles behind the Valac.

"Lock and fire all weapons," Farold ordered. "Helm, open a tunnel. Get us out of here."

Missiles whooshed from their tubes.

The forward railgun rumbled the operations center.

The flash of the particle beam cut across the enemy fleet.

Several Valac ships rolled end-to-end out of control.

"Admiral, our Mage Tunnel is opening."

"All ships continue firing while in normal space," Farold ordered over the ethercomm. "Rendezvous at position beta."

The fleet returned to normal space over half a Geller from the Devon star. The remote, nondescript location allowed the fleet time to assess their situation.

Farold met with his senior staff in a cramped conference compartment on the *Rubicon*. The off-site fleet captains attended via vid web.

"Most of our stealth probes remain active. They report eight Valac warships incurred heavy damage during out attack. Another ten received moderate or light damage."

The engineering officer slapped the conference table. "That's a good first attack."

"What damage did our ships incur?" Farold asked.

"Two ships sustained heavy damage during the attack." The intelligence officer turned to a holoview display rising from the center of the conference table. "Three other ships suffered moderate damage and are unable to jump. Those three are moving away and, for now, the Valac are ignoring all five."

"Are they continuing toward Exeter?" Captain Marin of the Argonaut asked.

"Yes," the *Rubicon* intelligence officer replied. "They'll be able to begin orbital bombardment in about twenty minutes."

"We caught the Valac by surprise this time. We won't have that luxury again." Farold stood.

Everyone came to attention.

"Adjust our jump angle to return to normal space high and behind the Valac fleet. During this next attack I want to inflict even greater pain. Execute part two of the battle plan. We jump in ten minutes" He turned his head slowly as he repeated the line from the anthem. "We are the point of the sword."

"Victory our only reward," everyone said in response. "Dismissed."

After everyone had left, Farold sat. The Orion warships would accelerate out of the tunnels, fire all weapons as they passed, and then disappear behind the enemy fleet as his warships dashed over the Exeter horizon. While out of sight, they would jump. That would provide little data about their eventual location to the Valac.

How long could they keep up this attack and retreat strategy?

"Retreat," Farold mumbled the hated word. But would the Valac retreat? Would help arrive? Both seemed unlikely outcomes. Farold sighed and returned to the bridge.

A new cup of tea cooled beside the command chair. Farold stared at the holoview as the Mage Tunnels formed and the fleet flew into battle.

Collision alarms sounded as the *Rubicon* returned to normal space. The *Hastings* filled the holoview display.

"Reverse thrust," the navigation officer ordered.

Three Valac dreadnaughts stood between them and other enemy vessels.

"Lock and fire all weapons." Farold stood and walked to the holoview as the *Hastings* shrunk in perspective and more enemy warships came into view.

The Valac fleet accelerated and dispersed.

Missiles launched and the railgun boomed like the beat of a drum.

"Wasps!" a young sensor tech shouted with fear in his voice.

The Valac equivalent of darts, Farold had already seen them as they swarmed around the lead Orion dreadnought. "Tell the particle beam gunner to target the wasps."

The navigation officer turned to Farold. "The *Hastings* is rolling out of control. We need to change course and—"

"Do it." Farold cursed softly. The Valac had been ready for them. "Keep accelerating. If we stay too long the Valac will—"

A thunderous explosion rocked the ship.

Alarms sounded.

Pain tore through Farold's leg. He looked down at a long jagged cut. His ears popped and he felt faint. A cloud of tea formed in the air as the cup beside him fell, gently tapped the deck, and then bounced back through the russet cloud.

Another blast shook the *Rubicon*.

Farold floated into the air, trailing blood in a scarlet arc.

*   *   *

Devon system, Planet Exeter

Rage on a scale he had never before experienced erupted within Lucas. He surged forward, arms outstretched, grasping for Alton's throat.

Behind the counter, Katherine crawled away. "Sarah, sound the house alarm!"

Alton fired at Lucas.

Alarms sounded.

The shot tore into Lucas's left prosthetic arm. Pain ripped along the limb. Sparks flew, and the device went limp at his side. Lucas slammed his knee into Alton's groin.

A painful groan escaped from Alton as he collapsed to the ground.

"Sarah, send a doctor to the armory." Katherine scurried along the floor and grabbed Alton's lance. "Send guards."

Lucas slammed his right fist into Alton's face, and blood gushed from the butler's broken nose. Then Lucas pressed his knee against the man's sternum, hoping to break bones. His prosthetic fingers grabbed Alton's neck and squeezed. Only when Alton lost consciousness did Lucas realize both Rachel and Katherine were yanking on him and shouting.

"Don't kill him!" Katherine wailed. "Why? Why did he do it? I need to know!" Tears ran down her cheeks.

"Is mother dead?" Lucas asked

Katherine ran to her mother, cradled her head, and screamed.

Lucas tightened his grip on Alton's throat, but couldn't maintain it. He felt drained and exhausted, but beyond that, it seemed like he was a ghost watching events while not a part of them.

"Are you okay?" Blood smeared Rachel's hands and dress.

"Yes." Lucas pointed to the blood. "Are you?"

Rachel nodded. "I tried to help your mother."

Tybalt, followed by a dozen marines, burst into the room. "What happened?"

"Alton shot my mother." Lucas said the words, but felt numb.

"By the God of Earth, why?" Tybalt knelt beside the body.

Lucas shook his head. "Take Alton to the medical wing and guard him. I need him alive. Sarah, silence the house alarms."

Dr. Meredith rushed in, hurried to Lady Charlotte, and retrieved emergency gear from his bag. As the marines hauled the unconscious Alton from the armory, the doctor examined the head and brain function of Lady Charlotte. Dr. Meredith's face paled and he shook his head. "The bullet traveled through—"

Katherine burst into sobs.

"I'm sorry." Dr. Meredith bit his lip. "Your mother is gone."

Lucas grabbed a hand lance from the rack and stared down the hall where the marines had taken Alton.

"I know what you're thinking." Rachel shook her head and clutched his hand. "I understand wanting revenge on Alton, but we need to know why he shot your mother." Rachel glanced at Lady Charlotte's body. "How many years has Alton been with your family?"

"All my life." As if turned into a statue, Lucas stared at his dead mother and crying sister, without feeling or movement.

"It doesn't make sense." Rachel shook her head.

"We'll get answers from Alton. Then we'll feed him to the Valac." He watched his weeping sister and wondered why his own tears didn't come. He should've felt something, but he remained cold. He looked to Rachel. "Take care of Katherine, please. Get Naomi to help you. I do want answers, but there's still a war to fight."

* * *

Lucas winced as the Dr. Meredith attached a replacement arm. He flexed his new prosthetic fingers, eager to again dig them into Alton's neck.

"You need to rest and heal," the doctor said.

Without a word Lucas stood and left still flexing his fingers. In his bedroom he dressed in full combat armor, except the helmet. Then he gathered his weapons and returned to the hospital wing.

Just over an hour had passed when Lucas stood alongside the still unconscious murderer of his mother.

The door whooshed open, and Tybalt entered, also ready for combat. "The battle isn't going well. We don't have much time."

Lucas turned to Dr. Meredith. "Wake him."

The doctor pressed the injector against Alton's neck. "His voice will be impaired from your chokehold."

Lucas didn't care.

Alton's eyes popped open, and he struggled against the chain restraints. Then he gazed at Meredith, Tybalt, and finally focused on Lucas.

"Why did you kill my mother?"

"Water." Alton struggled to say the word.

Dr. Meredith poured him a glass, but Lucas waved off the delivery and repeated his question.

Alton looked away.

"I could kill you here and now. There would be an inquest, but I'd never be convicted of anything."

Without turning his face, Alton said, "Your entire family has already been convicted."

"What nonsense is that?" Lucas asked. "If all you have are the words of a lunatic, I should just kill you now."

"Prince Draven told me of your family's treason." Alton's gravelly voice rasped.

Lucas grabbed Alton by his jaw and stared into his face. "What treason is that?"

"He said you found a crazy girl that claims to be from Earth, that you were using her to break the alliance between us and the Mage."

Lucas released Alton like he would a dirty rag. "And what part of this supposed treason did my mother play?"

"The prince said you were all sentenced to death. I was to ensure the sentence was carried out, and if I did, my son would never serve on the front again."

"Sarah, do you have this all recorded?"

She appeared in the center of the room. "Yes, Lord Lucas."

"Good." Lucas turned and shot Alton between the eyes.

Chapter 14

Orion Fleet on Station in
the Devon System

Farold awoke on the deck. Emergency lights illuminated an otherwise dark compartment. A muffled voice came to him. "The Admiral is dead."

Two men stumbled past him. "Come with us or you'll be dead, too."

"His eyes …" The journalist leaned over Farold. "… I think they blinked."

The other two disappeared from view.

Farold gasped and pushed himself up against the command chair. The ship shuddered, and overhead lights flickered. The consoles before him indicated the ship was on emergency power and that it would soon fail.

"They ordered abandon ship." The journalist shouted, waved, and pointed. "We've got to go."

"Who gave the order?" Farold struggled to grasp the situation. The operations center stood nearly empty. Two bodies stained with blood lay on the deck nearby. The only other living person was the journalist with his vid recorder strapped near his shoulder.

Lights blinked and flickered. Alarms blared. "I'm the commanding officer. Only I can give the order to abandon ship. Where is everyone?"

"They thought you were dead." The journalist shook his head. "I'm not sure who gave the order, but everyone is either dead or gone." He pointed to the holoview. "Look! We're spinning out of control."

The blue and green orb of Exeter shot across the screen, and then only stars and wreckage littered the black void. Exeter again came into view for a moment, and then stars and wreckage returned. Exeter grew larger with each spin of the vessel.

"We've got to abandon ship now!" The journalist pulled on Farold's arm.

Farold spotted no Valac warships but knew they remained in orbit, probably bombarding the far side of the planet. They would return, and his ship couldn't fight. He struggled to stand as pain tore along his calf. Bile climbed his throat. "My leg is wounded."

"I can see that." The journalist reached out his arm.

Farold gripped his arm, stood, and teetered on one foot while he grasped the journalist's shoulder. The journalist held Farold at the waist, and together they crept toward the passageway.

Dizzy and unable to put much weight on his limb, Farold struggled to provide coherent directions to the launch bay.

In the passageways, only flashing red alarms and dim emergency lights lit their way. Despite using every pipe, ledge, and knob to speed their journey down three levels, Farold might've been able to crawl faster.

When they neared the launch bay, the doors didn't open.

The ship rumbled and shrieked.

"Has it lost atmosphere?" The journalist's eyes flared wide. "Are we stranded?"

"Perhaps not. The doors lock as a safety measure, but there's another way in." Farold pointed down the passageway to a hatch. "If you can open it, the pressure in the bay is adequate."

The hatch, dogged down for battle, didn't readily open. Both men, pushed, pulled, and grunted on the wheel.

Standing on one leg, with sweat pouring down his face, Farold couldn't help much.

Finally, the door budged and creaked open.

With one arm on Farold's waist, the journalist stepped sideways through the hatch. "Step over the frame."

A thousand knives seemed to cut into him when Farold leaned onto his injured leg. Beads of sweat rolled down his face as he stepped into the compartment.

Only three darts remained on the launch rails.

Metal scraped and screeched. A breeze blew across the bay.

They hurried toward the lead craft.

Climbing the ramp proved nearly impossible for Farold, so he leaned into the journalist and hopped up and into the vehicle. When they reached the controls, the journalist plopped Farold into the navigation seat.

Farold started to protest, but between the pain and dizziness, he thought better of it. He sighed, strapped himself in, and wiped blood and sweat from his forehead. "What's your name?"

"Huh?" The journalist latched his harness.

"I thought I was the one hit on the head." Farold pulled the medical kit from a nearby drawer. "Your name? I never bothered to learn it."

"Brian West. Ah ... where is ... oh, here." The catapult hurled the dart down the rail, through the launch tube, and into the blackness of space. Weightlessness overtook the craft.

Tiny crimson drops floated from Farold's leg and head.

Brian leaned forward and pressed two red buttons simultaneously.

"Emergency evacuation automatos controls engaging," a mechanical voice announced.

Three seconds later, thrusters fired and the craft made a tight turn. The yellow Devon sun shone into the dart for a moment, and then the blue of an Exeter Ocean came into view.

From experience, Farold knew that automatos systems would use speed as a defense. The detectors set them on course for Exeter. They'd shoot toward the planet like a meteor falling from the sky and at the last moment, they'd level off and land somewhere. It would be a short, but heart-pounding ride.

As the blackness gave way to dark blue, Farold wrapped his head with a bandage. "Where's your family?"

"My mother and the rest of my relatives are on Brittany." Brian frowned. "My father died in the battle of Orkney."

"I fought in that battle as a young lieutenant. I wonder if I met your father." He patted Brian on the shoulder. "I'm glad your family is safe." Farold sighed. "Change course and land at the Camden Operations Center."

"Is your family there?"

"Yes, and if today is the day I die, I'd like to do so with them."

Brian nodded, changed course, and soon Camden Peak came into view. "This is going to be a great vid story—if we live."

*   *   *

Lucas stared as the blood dripped from Alton's head to the floor. Dr. Meredith stumbled back against the wall, his mouth open and eyes wide.

"There are less incriminating ways to kill a man." Tybalt scowled. "We could have ordered him to scout Valac positions. If Prince Draven hears of this, he'll have the legal right to arrest you."

"I'll deal with him later, if I'm not killed in battle, or arrested by Nightwatch." Lucas holstered his lance. "I suggest we go to my father's office. You can use his ethercomm systems to contact the operations center and deploy the men."

Tybalt turned to the doctor. "You've been making preparations for the battle and were never in this room."

Dr. Meredith nodded and hurried away.

Lucas's anger flowed as he followed Tybalt out the door. "What do we do with the body?"

"*We'll* be doing nothing," Tybalt said. "Add that task to the list of things *you'll* be dealing with—if you survive the battle."

"Yes, sir." So many emotions jumbled in his mind that he felt confused and drained. He wanted to be alone to sort his thoughts, but he knew that would be impossible until the battle had been won. Thoughts of his mother, dead on the floor, pushed into his mind.

He shook his head. Now was not the time for mourning. That time would come after the battle, and when he was alone. He rubbed his face and eyes.

"Did Alton talk? What did he say?" Katherine asked.

At the sound of her voice, Lucas turned. He stood near her and Tybalt on the top floor of the mansion.

Tybalt glanced at Lucas, but they both remained silent.

Finally Tybalt found voice. "He admitted to working for Prince Draven and Nightwatch. Alton's mission was to ensure everyone in the Baldwin family died today."

"Well, he should die before any more of my family does."

Tybalt nodded. "I think we can be certain that will happen."

"Good." Katherine wiped tears from her face. "Mother's bod—" She choked. "Uh, she's been moved to a spare room." She shook her head. "I'm going to get a battle lance. Are you two headed to father's office?"

"Yes," Tybalt said.

"I'll see you there in a few minutes." Katherine hurried away.

Lucas thought about ordering her to go to the blast shelter, but knew she wouldn't. He was proud of her. In some ways, she was stronger than him.

"Lucas, come on." Tybalt waved from twenty feet ahead. "We need to make final plans."

*   *   *

Earlier, Katherine had strapped a hand lance to one leg, but now she wanted something more powerful. She hurried to the armory in the basement. Five marines in the room gathered lances and ammunition. She avoided looking at the crimson stain on the floor. Rachel sat in the corner and stared in Katherine's direction with unfocused eyes.

As Katherine reached for the last battle lance on the rack, so did a young marine. She snarled, "This one's mine."

The marine jerked his hand back.

Katherine grabbed the weapon, and hurried from the armory back up the stairs. She knew the wing where they had Alton taken, but not the room. "Sarah, where is Alton being held?"

"His last recorded position is three doors down on the left, but I no longer detect him."

When the door opened, she immediately spotted the cuff and chain.

She had never killed a living thing, but still she hoped to avenge her mother's death.

Several years ago a man had been flogged for theft in the town center. She had hurried around the corner just as the first blow was delivered. Never would she forget the crack of the whip, the torn flesh, or the thief's screams. She had stared, unable to shift her eyes from the bloody sight as the next lash ripped across his back. Then her bodyguard had shuffled her away.

In a similar manner, she had once come upon a man still hanging from the gallows. For a moment she had stared into the man's lifeless eyes, and again, a bodyguard hurried her away. At the time, she thought it impossible for her to crack the whip or release the gallows trapdoor, but now, filled with rage, she raised her lance and stepped closer to Alton.

Blood dripped into a growing pool on the floor.

She edged forward until she stared into Alton's lifeless eyes. Revulsion mixed with relief that the killer of her mother was dead. But who had done the deed?

Lucas and Tybalt had both been reluctant to answer her questions about Alton. Had one of them shot him? It didn't matter. The battle hadn't gone well. It was likely they would all soon be dead.

Chapter 15

Devon System, Planet Exeter

Farold slammed the injector into his leg as the dart continued to arc toward the ground. He had no idea what further damage he might've done to the limb by walking on it. If it had to be removed and regrown, well, he could consider that later, after the battle. For now, he needed to stand and fight. He sighed as the painkillers took effect and began wrapping the leg in a bandage.

"We can't land at Camden Peak." Brian shook his head. "The landing tubes have been blasted, and all the auto-landing systems are down." Red dots littered the detector screen.

"Go here." Farold tapped on the display and continued to bandage his leg.

Brian squinted at the screen. "Camden House?"

"Land on the roof."

"At the speed we're going?" Brian struggled with the controls as he talked. "I'm barely flying this thing. I can't land it on a roof, not even a big one like Camden House."

"I'll do it." Farold finished wrapping his leg.

"Oh, that's a great idea. How many injections have you given yourself?"

Farold scowled. "Enough to make me certain that I can do it, but not enough to ignore your insolence."

Brian gritted his teeth and let Farold take the controls.

*   *   *

Rachel sat in the corner of the armory trying to understand all the horrid events since she awoke on Lepeus Delta. There, tortured by the Auxilium and used in some sort of experiment, she had first encountered the Valac when they attacked the planet.

She ran terrified from the Valac until Lucas found and shot her. Then, she awoke in the brig.

She fought the Valac on the Argonaut and later on Katherine's ship. Several times, she'd heard the strange, depressing song of the Valac, and today it grew even louder in her head.

Then moments ago, she happened upon Katherine's murdered mother. Rachel looked across the room. People sped back and forth as they handed out weapons, but they avoided the large red stain on the floor.

As if to cap off the tumultuous events of her recent life, the battle now raging in space would determine if she'd live or die. She'd heard once that God didn't burden people with more temptation than they could bear, but what about worry and strife? She had gone to church many times, but never really paid attention. Now she wished she knew more, but there was no place, no time, to learn. Tears ran down her cheeks. The huge weight of would crush her soul.

Had the Earth been destroyed? Maybe not, but would she ever see it, or her family, again? Would she die today? She had many questions but no answers. She wanted to hide somewhere and wait for the nightmare to end.

"Excuse me, Miss Rachel." Anna stepped close with two battle lances. "They're handing out weapons to everyone, even the women."

Rachel stood and took the lance.

"They want the women to go to the blast shelter in the basement."

"Why?"

Anna frowned and tilted her head. "Because we're women, I suppose. The men are setting up defensive positions in the mountain, nearby bunkers and fortified parts of the house."

"I've got some questions to ask before I sit here and wait to die." She slung the battle lance over her shoulder. "Is there a church nearby?"

"A church?" Anna shook her head. "Not like a big church or cathedral, but there's a small chapel behind the house. Shall I show you?"

She shook her head. "Sarah can direct me. I'll rejoin you in a few minutes."

Rachel returned to the main floor, and as she crossed the foyer, she called upon Sarah to lead her to the chapel.

Light shimmered and Sarah appeared. "Follow me, Miss Rachel."

When they stood just inside the servant's entrance at the rear of the house, Sarah pointed and her arm reached out the door and disappeared.

"The Baldwin family chapel is just beyond the bend in the path," she said. "There are no holo projectors, so I can't lead you there."

"That's okay." Rachel forced a grin. "I can find it from here."

With a curtsy, Sarah disappeared.

Rachel wanted to be alone, but she didn't feel alone. Soldiers scurried nearby, and the Valac song resounded in her mind. She ran the narrow gravel path to the chapel.

The brown, stone building stood larger than she expected. With stained glass windows and a steeple, it looked like an English village church. With some snow, the image would've made a festive a Christmas card. She pulled on one of the large wooden doors and it swung open.

Eight rows of pews stood on the right and left. The stained glass windows contained images of humans, Aux, and strange, warrior-like angels. A pulpit and altar stood on a platform at the far end. Above it, a large cross carving decorated the support beams. Above it all, carved near the ceiling, loomed a globe that might've been Earth.

As she rushed forward, memories of candlelight services at Christmas, Easter in a new dress, and youth events with friends, flashed through her mind.

Rachel knelt at the altar and set the battle lance down in front of her. "God, I don't know if you can even hear me from this faraway place. Am I going insane, God?"

The Valac song thundered in her mind.

Distant blasts rattled the windows.

"I don't want to die. Help me live. Help me find a way home."

Explosions splintered the wooden doors and shattered the windows.

Valac burst into the church.

Rachel jumped to her feet and screamed.

The girth of the Valac made it impossible for them to enter through the shattered stained glass windows, but Valac stood in each, with the stingers of their tails swaying overhead. Dust floated in the air from the splintered wooden doors. The open frame now provided ample area for the eight-legged monsters to enter.

A line of Valac marched into the church and up the aisle toward her with their song resounding off the stone walls.

With trembling fingers she snatched the battle lance from the altar, and dashed out a back door, through a cemetery of tall stone monuments, and into the forest. She sprinted through trees she hoped were close enough together to prevent the Valac from pursuing her. Racing left and right through the tightest spaces, she swung back toward the house.

As she ran out of the forest near the mansion, a boom rattled the glass of the windows. Rachel looked skyward. A dart, under fire from the Valac, landed with a thud on the roof of Camden House. Rachel hoped the dart held reinforcements.

"Sarah, open the servants' entrance!" Rachel shouted and prayed to be heard. The door swung open, and she rushed in. "Sarah, shut it … lock it!"

Her breaths rapid, Rachel stumbled forward, deeper into the house. Then she turned and aimed the battle lance at the door and waited for several moments.

The Valac couldn't have entered through the narrow hall. They might blast their way in, but none did. Their song still reached her mind, though, and stirred emotions of sadness and dread within her.

Rachel sprinted along empty halls looking for Lucas and Katherine. In the main foyer, a large group of marines moved heavy furniture to make a barricade.

"Where's Lucas?"

"Cornet Baldwin? Top floor. The admiral's office, assisting the lieutenant." The man pointed. "But you should be with the other women in the basement."

"Is that where Lady Katherine is?"

He shrugged. "I would suppose."

She doubted Katherine was huddling in the basement. Rachel slung her battle lance over one shoulder and hurried up the stairs. Breathless, she arrived at the office and walked through the open door.

Several men glanced in her direction, but none said anything. Lucas and Tybalt stood with their backs to her. As expected, Katherine was there, standing in a corner with a battle lance over one shoulder. She might not be in the basement, but everyone seemed to ignore her.

It surprised her to see Farold standing behind his desk, and the persistent journalist from earlier in the far corner of the room. She thought they'd both left with the fleet. Perhaps they had.

The journalist appeared dazed, and Farold stood in a torn, bloodstained uniform, with bandages around his head and leg.

Rachel moved beside Katherine. "Is your father okay? Didn't he go into space with the fleet?"

"He arrived moments ago." Katherine frowned. "I think he'll be okay, but … well …." She bit her lip. "Him being here, like that, can't be a good thing."

"Do they know that Valac are outside the house?"

Katherine nodded.

Lucas glanced at Rachel. His face softened for a moment, but then he turned away.

The holoview snapped on, displaying an officer in front of the desk. "I'm glad to see you're alive, Admiral. The Rubicon fell from orbit a few minutes ago. Is Camden House under attack?"

"Not yet. The Valac are outside, but they haven't fired on it yet. We're not sure why. What's the status of the fleet?"

"Thirty-seven ships remain effective combatants and are currently regrouping for another attack run."

Farold nodded. "I had hoped to remain with the fleet longer and allow planetary defenses more time to target the Valac ships. Neither appears to have been effective."

The officer shook his head. "The Valac fleet are in an elongated orbit so they come in low over this continent and avoid planetary defenses on other parts of Exeter. Likewise, their attacks have focused on defensive positions in this region. Over a thousand Valac wasps have landed in the Camden Peak area."

Rachel shuddered at the thought of so many Valac nearby.

While Farold continued to talk about attack angles and weapons with the officer, Rachel's attention turned to Lucas and Tybalt.

"The Valac don't often land, do they?" Lucas asked.

"No." Tybalt shook his head. "Usually, they bombard a planet from orbit."

"That's what I thought." Lucas stared at a holo projection of the region. "They're ignoring the cities and surrounding the Camden Peak area. Why do you think they landed this time?"

Tybalt shrugged. "Perhaps they want something."

Lucas and Katherine both glanced at Rachel.

She knew what the Valac wanted. Lucas and Katherine might not want to admit it, but they knew, too. The Valac had attacked the planet in search of her. Their song and the feelings it invoked rose within Rachel as more of them circled the house. Somehow, she knew that she needed to go to them, or their song would just continue and grow louder, both on the air and in her head.

She stood and mumbled, "I've got to go."

"Where?" Katherine asked.

Rachel gave no answer. Instead, she hurried from the room and headed down the stairs. As she neared the main doors a marine called to her from the barricade. "What are you doing?"

"Just stepping outside." Rachel swiped the door with her bracelet, great steel bars slid back, and she pulled it open. "You should probably lock this behind me just in case my plan doesn't work."

Then she ran out.

Chapter 16

Devon system, Planet Exeter

Farold turned to Tybalt. "I'm leaving. Hold this position as long as you can and then fall back to the operations center."

"Look!" Lucas banged on the window.

"What?" Farold cast his son an annoyed glance.

Lucas banged the glass again.

Farold joined Lucas at the window. Outside, Rachel stood alone at the top of the walkway. Hundreds of Valac formed an arc along the front of the house. A dozen more Valac pushed toward Rachel.

The Valac song crescendoed so loud that it reverberated through the room.

"I've got to save her!" Lucas ran for the door.

"No!" Farold reached out to stop him, but Lucas dashed from the room. "Tybalt, you have command of this position. Brian, help me down the stairs."

The journalist clamped the vid recorder on his arm and assisted Farold.

In the hallway, Farold called to his son over the ethercomm. "Lucas, do *not* leave this building."

"I've got to, or they'll kill her."

"I don't think so."

"What? Why would you think that? I—I can't risk it. I'm going to get her."

"Wait for me. We'll get her together."

Silence passed for a moment.

"Be quick, Father."

"I will." Farold and Brian continued down, but on the top of the last flight of stairs Farold stopped and injected more painkillers. He turned to Brian. "Don't assist me, or even look like you might, unless I stumble."

Then Farold limped down the stairs, hoping that his face displayed only stoic calm.

In the foyer, Lucas waited by the door. Farold drew close to him and whispered, "Cornet Baldwin, we will speak of your insubordination later—if we live."

Lucas nodded.

Farold turned to the marines behind the barricade. "Lieutenant, you and ten of your men stay behind. The rest assemble alongside me."

The marines gathered around Farold.

"The Valac haven't attacked the house yet, and I'm hoping they don't. We're going to try to retrieve that girl just outside without any shooting. So, if the Valac shoot, return fire, but otherwise do not engage unless I give the order. Does everyone understand that?"

"Yes, Admiral," echoed throughout the foyer.

With a slow turn, Farold gazed into the eyes of each man. "Okay, we move out slow and easy." Farold grabbed the door handle. "Remember, hold your fire. Sarah, unlock and open this door."

With lances ready, the men crept from the house as a group.

The Valac formed an arc from one side of the house to the other with Rachel thirty feet ahead.

"Marines, stay together and with me." Farold eased forward. "Rachel, can you hear me?"

The entire world seemed to vibrate in unison with the Valac song. Dozens of them scrambled along the front of the house, closing the circle around the humans.

Lucas stepped past his father. "Rachel, come to me."

"They're surrounding us," a young marine shouted.

"I can see that." Farold inched closer. "Rachel, we need to get back inside."

Lucas stepped beside Rachel. "It's like she's in a trance."

The Valac closed the circle around the humans. Rachel stood at the center with Farold facing her on the left and Lucas on the right. Brian knelt nearby with the vid recorder now in front of his face. Beyond them stood of ring of about forty marines, surrounded by hundreds of Valac with their stingers dancing overhead.

The Valac song stopped as one crept forward.

Several marines targeted their lances.

"Let him … let it through," Farold ordered.

The marines stepped back.

The lone Valac edged forward. Its claw-like feet clicked on the stones of the porch.

Farold had never been so close to so many Valac, and now one inched ever closer. He wanted to shoot it. He glanced at the marines around him and knew the situation could easily erupt into violence. "Lances down. Point your lances at the ground, now."

After every marine obeyed, the Valac lowered their stingers.

The color of the lone Valac seemed to fade as it approached.

When it stood less than ten feet away Farold held up his hand. "Okay," he said in a calm voice. "What do you want?"

The creature swayed back and forth.

"Are you here to kill or to talk?" Farold stared into the compound eyes that ran along either side of the Valac's frontal carapace.

"Talk."

Farold twisted back at the sound of a human voice.

The Valac scurried back several steps as its plates darkened.

Farold took a slow step toward Rachel. Had the monotone word come from her?

After several moments the Valac's plates lightened to a dark, almost navy blue, and it shuffled forward, its talons again clicking on the stones. With one claw-like hand, it reached out and touched Rachel's head.

She stiffened and her eyes rolled back, leaving only a white orb visible.

Lucas reached for her, but Farold stayed his son's hand.

Rachel's muscles relaxed, but her eyes remained unchanged. She swayed in unison with the Valac and reached out with one hand, mimicking its claw. "For many generations we have sought a way to speak with the human slaves of the Mage."

The lone Valac now had a definite blue color as it hummed softly.

Rachel continued to whisper the Valac thoughts. "Once before we spoke, and, for a time, the attacks stopped."

Struggling to hear every word, Farold stepped closer to Rachel and the blue Valac.

"Now we have found another who can speak for us. We are not your enemy. We did not destroy your world."

While he knew the Valac words were true, Farold needed absolute proof that he could set before the Privy Council and nobles. If he had anything less, another civil war would result. "How can I prove this?"

"We were once the slaves of the Mage. We once fought for them. We broke free."

"But, how can I prove what you say is true?"

"We see the truth within the one you call Rachel. Listen. See. We will leave before your warships return. Your actions will inform us."

Before Farold could ask another question, the blue Valac stepped back.

Rachel slumped.

Lucas caught her.

The blue Valac merged with the others. All of them appeared to be lighter in color as they moved away.

"Keep your lances down." Farold ordered. "Don't fire unless you're fired upon."

Within seconds, no Valac remained in sight.

"Take care of Rachel," Farold said to Lucas. Then he hurried to the operations center and ordered a system wide ceasefire.

Over the next hour, every Valac ship left the Devon and Efford systems.

*　　*　　*

Rachel awoke in darkness. Panic surged through her until she recognized the carvings of the four-poster bed and the pattern of the comforter. This was her room in Camden House.

She released a long slow breath and struggled to remember what had happened. Everything was clear until she had left the house. Then it all seemed like a dream. Thankfully, the Valac song no longer resounded in her mind.

A snore came from a dark corner of the room.

Rachel pushed back the covers. Someone had changed her into a long nightgown. She stood and inched toward the dark corner.

Another rattling snore broke the stillness of the night. Anna slept in a nearby chair.

Moonlight flowed in from the balcony. Rachel wandered into the light and the night air. High in the sky, one small moon hung near another larger one.

"Castor, the smaller moon, orbits Pollux."

Rachel gasped.

Lucas stood on the next balcony.

"I didn't see you," she frowned. "Wouldn't a gentleman announce their presence?"

"Forgive me. I couldn't sleep and just stepped out on the balcony."

She smiled inwardly. Lucas hadn't noticed the sarcasm in her Jane Austin-like etiquette question. "Why are you there? That's not your room."

"I wanted to be nearby when you woke. Are you okay?"

"A little confused, but yes, I believe I'm fine." She smiled. "Would you like to come over?"

"That would be indecorous."

"I'll wake Anna." Rachel grinned. "If you act improperly, she'll defend my virtue."

"Then I would enjoy the pleasure of your company."

Rachel tugged on her gown. "I'll send Anna when I'm more properly dressed."

By the time Anna returned with Lucas, Rachel had the news up on a vid screen.

"Do you remember what happened yesterday on the front steps?" Lucas asked.

Rachel shook her head. "Not clearly. I'm not even sure how much time has passed."

"A little more than twelve hours."

She sat on one end of a small couch and motioned for Lucas to sit on the other. "I'm trying to remember, but it all seems like a dream." She glanced at the screen. "Sarah, increase the vid volume."

"… and against incredible odds, the Terran forces under command of Lord Admiral Baldwin halted the Valac advance and saved Exeter and the entire Devon system."

Anna shook her head. "Several of the men told us that you talked with the Valac. That you touched one, and it changed color."

"That's not exactly how it happened." Lucas shook his head. "I was there, with my father."

"What did he do?" Anna stared at Lucas.

Lucas stood and his face flushed.

Rachel leaned over and grasped his hand.

"Miss Rachel was the first one there." Anna stepped back and her voice wavered. "She touched them, spoke with them, and made them leave."

Still holding onto Lucas, Rachel shook her head and tried to remember what had happened.

"You saved us." Anna bowed her head and curtsied to Rachel. "You are the foretold Daughter of Earth. You'll protect all the Seekers and lead us to freedom."

"Insolence does not become you, Anna." Lucas glared. "Change is coming, but be careful, or we may all die before it arrives."

Chapter 17

Devon system, Planet Exeter

Rachel released Lucas's hand and waved Anna away. "You can go now. I'll call when I need you."

When Anna had left, Lucas shook his head. "Perhaps I should leave also."

"Not just yet." She tapped the couch beside her. "Sit for just a minute." When he did, she continued. "It's been a long day for all of us. Don't hold Anna's words against her."

"She needs to be more discrete, or she'll at least anger Father, and that would be bad enough. He has been very angry since the battle. At worst, she might get us all killed." He breathed deep and let it out. "It's clear you're very important to the Valac. I don't understand all that happened earlier today. Father asked questions, and you seemed to speak for them."

"I did?"

"I was so tense … some of it's hazy." Lucas then told her all that he recalled.

"I remember some." Rachel nodded. "But it all seems more like a dream that's about to slip away." Realization dawned, and she turned to Lucas with her mouth agape. "They were looking for me. Out of all the humans they've encountered they were looking for me."

"Yes, it seems they were."

"Am I this Daughter of Earth?"

"Anna believes you are, and so does probably every other helot—Seeker—on the estate."

Rachel drew in a deep breath and let it out. "Anna said I saved them and would protect them and lead them to freedom." She shook her head. "I'm just a girl from Earth. I can't save or protect anyone."

"I'm not sure what will happen." Lucas shook his head. "But after seeing you talk for the Valac, anything might be possible."

"Me, leading people out of bondage like Moses? That's not possible."

*   *   *

A short time later, Lucas left Rachel and went to the room where Alton's body remained. Earlier in the evening he'd moved the body into a gravunit. Now, late at night, he would move it to the nearby forest and bury it.

He slid the first gravunit pole through the four rings that circled the casket like cylinder. It clicked into place. When he had done the same with the second pole the unit was ready for transport. Still, it would be difficult. The device was meant for use by at least two people.

The unit hummed as he turned the power up high. As he grabbed the poles on one end, the hair on his arms stood up. With a grunt, he lifted the unit. His prosthetic arms dug into his flesh as he maneuvered the device out of the room and down the hall. *I should have killed you on the first floor.*

Something moved in the shadows by the stairs. Lucas stopped and let the unit drop with a thud.

Tybalt stepped from the shadows. "Your father has been looking for you."

"I've been busy."

"Is that Alton's body in the gravunit?"

Lucas nodded.

"How did you say that he died?"

"I told father about mother's murder." He shook his head and felt the hate boil within him again. "Then I said we arrested Alton, but needed him to defend the house. He was sent out with a unit that was attacked. During the battle, he died."

"Here." Tybalt passed a palmcomp to Lucas. "He's listed as one of the dead from the battle here at the house. An entry has been made in his service record saying that he missed the sailing of the *Rubicon*. He later discovered your mother dead from an unknown assailant, possibly Valac. After that he fought with the marines here, died in action, and you approved his burial in space."

"He has family. They'll ask for his body."

"Not before the burial transport leaves in two hours." Tybalt shrugged. "When his grieving widow does ask for the body, you will need to apologize profusely."

"You want me to apologize to Alton's family and agree to a story that will mean he's never accountable as the murderer of my mother?"

"His family is not to blame. Prince Draven is, and if you had waited, someone acting on behalf of the royal family would have killed him." Tybalt shook his head. "Alton was never going to live through this. A loyal servant killing Lady Charlotte raises too many questions that no one wants to publically answer."

"What about the marines who were there?"

"None saw him kill her. The report says that Alton discovered Lady Charlotte's body, became hysterical, but later calmed down. He fought bravely in the battle but sadly died."

Lucas shook his head. "Who will believe this?"

"When you authorize the report, I'll follow. Then your father will give the final approval, and it will become the official record." Tybalt waved his hand. "All else is rumor and innuendo."

As he read the documents Tybalt had prepared, Lucas came to reluctant agreement. He held the unit near his face, and it scanned his eye for authorization. "This is a good plan. I never knew you were so cunning."

"This is your father's plan."

"What? How?"

"He didn't believe your story and came to me in search of the truth. Come on. Let's get this cylinder moved."

Less than an hour later, Alton's body was one of many waiting for burial in space in the operations center.

*   *   *

The next morning, Rachel walked with a tearful Katherine to the chapel behind the mansion. The stained glass windows and wood doors hadn't been fixed, but the building had been swept and cleaned. Where the altar had been, Lady Charlotte's casket now stood.

Tybalt motioned for Rachel to sit with him in the second row, behind the Baldwin family. She guessed that those beside Tybalt were his parents. Anna and Naomi stood in the back. From Farold on down to the humblest private, all the men were in uniform. All the women and children wore black.

After several minutes of waiting, Rachel leaned over to Tybalt and whispered, "Is a priest coming?"

"A vicar, yes. He'll be here shortly."

Rachel nodded and added "vicar" to the list of strange words she needed to remember.

Among the mourners, about fifteen children stood in the back. Where had they come from? There were no children in the house. She leaned toward Tybalt, about to ask, when somber music filled the air.

The door Rachel had escaped through yesterday opened, and a man in black priestly robes entered. He walked to the central point behind the casket and raised his head. "The Earth is no more, but heaven is eternal and untouched by this sinful universe. May the God of Earth find the soul of Lady Charlotte in this foreign land, and carry her home."

The vicar spoke more, but Rachel heard little. Instead, memories of her own family flooded her mind. A cool breeze through the broken windows brought a memory of Christmas as she and her brother Reilly ran, pushing each other to be the first to the Christmas tree and presents. Would she ever see him or her parents again?

Other memories of friends and Earth filled her thoughts.

Earth.

So many thought it was gone, but Rachel knew from Prince Draven, and now from the Valac, that it remained out there, somewhere.

Only when she heard "amen" did her thoughts return to the chapel. As everyone stood, she hurried to follow.

"I've got to stay here," Tybalt said. "Follow the others out."

Hoping to avoid strangers, Rachel slipped to the side of the chapel. Anna and Naomi both smiled when she exited with them, but Rachel just wanted to be near familiar faces.

A steel framework, something like a bedframe, surrounded a grave. Also like a bedframe, each corner had a post, but these stood only three feet tall and had a U-shaped groove at the top. Farold, Katherine, and Lucas sat in chairs along one side of the open grave.

Acting as pallbearers, Tybalt and three other officers came around the church. Each held the end of a pole at shoulder-height. The poles ran through a set of four rings, and Lady Charlotte's casket hovered within them.

From the way the four held the poles, the weight seemed less than Rachel expected. As they passed her, she heard a hum, and her hair drifted toward the casket.

Did the rings affect gravity around the coffin like the gravbed did for medical patients?

The pallbearers set the poles in the grooves of the posts, and the vicar moved to the head of the grave. He offered more prayers and concluded by opening a small container. "From the dust of Earth we came, but we shall return to the dust of the stars." He sprinkled something over the grave as the rings opened, and as if by magic, the casket slid through the air into the ground below.

As the others departed, Rachel walked among the large gravestones that marked over a hundred years of the Baldwin family on this planet. Back on Earth, she'd only been in a cemetery twice. Both times she'd read the headstones as she walked and she did here as well. One of the newer gray stones bore a fresh engraving: Lady Elizabeth Baldwin, Wife of Lord Farold Baldwin and mother of Viscount Victor.

The Victor mentioned on the stone had to refer to Lucas and Katherine's older brother. She'd never met Victor and never thought about the distance in ages between them. It seemed from the engraving that Victor was a half-brother. An interesting tidbit about her hosts, but unimportant. Rachel strolled back toward the house.

Food for the guests lined the large table in the dining room, but Rachel wasn't hungry. Farold, Lucas, and Katherine stood stiff and stoic nearby. When people greeted the siblings and offered sympathy, they responded, but it all seemed mechanical to Rachel.

Several hours later, she managed to get Katherine in a quiet corner of the room. "You look tired. Do you need to stay? Leave and go rest?"

Katherine took a deep breath. "It's my place now to stand in for mother on formal occasions."

"Really?" Rachel frowned. "Surely today no one would blame you for leaving."

"You hardly knew Mother." Katherine frowned. "No one expects you to remain."

"I'll stay for you."

Katherine shook her head. "I've got to help Father."

Rachel stayed until the first guests left. Then she followed them from the somber home and walked into the gardens. Since Katherine had first shown her around, Rachel had wanted to spend more time here. She admired the strange, colorful flowers and bushes with green, yellow, blue, and purple leaves. She rounded a large orange bush with dozens of bright violet flowers and collided with Lucas.

"Oh, so sorry." He reached and caught her by the sleeve of her gown as she stumbled back into the bush.

"I thought you'd still be inside or off rebuilding the fleet or something."

"Father and Tybalt returned to duty an hour ago. I'm still on the injured list, but I needed to get out of the house and do something."

She nodded. "It seems we think alike."

"May I walk with you?"

"If you answer some questions for me."

"Of course." Lucas held out his arm.

Rachel recognized the gesture and wrapped her arm around his. Together, they continued in the direction she'd been going.

"Why aren't there any children in the mansion?"

"Because Katherine finally grew up."

"Oh, very funny. There were children in the chapel."

"They came from Camden village."

Rachel pictured a rural English village. "Is it nearby? I'd like to see it."

His eyes narrowed. "About a half-mile away. You really want to see it? Are you up to walking?"

"Yes, I'd love to go there, and I have both my legs. Are *you* up to it?"

He grinned. "It's this way."

They followed a wide gravel path to an ornate, yet broken iron gate.

"Did the Valac do this?" Rachel asked.

"Yes, and they blasted many spots along the wall also." Lucas turned to her with a serious look. "This is the only place in the entire Devon system where they landed soldiers."

The thought of giant beasts traversing trillions of miles for her sent a shudder through Rachel. She shuffled those fears to a dark corner of her mind. "What will happen to Alton?"

"He died during the battle and was buried in space this morning."

Rachel stared at Lucas expecting a more complete answer, but he provided none and she decided not to ask.

When they exited through the broken gate, the lane narrowed and turned into a simple dirt path through a forest of ancient trees.

"Do you think the war might be over?"

Lucas shook his head, and his face darkened. "I doubt it ever will be.

Remembering the headstone that mentioned Victor, and wanting to turn the conversation in a more pleasant direction, Rachel asked, "When will your brother return home?"

Lucas's face remained grim. "Soon. Father received word this morning."

"That doesn't make you happy?"

"We've never been close." He pointed. "The village is just around this next bend."

"Who lives there?"

"Mostly helots … uh, Seekers that work on the estate."

"Oh." Rachel struggled to imagine a Seeker village.

"The village is in the dell ahead."

The path straightened and sloped into a narrow valley. Just ahead, a simple wooden bridge spanned a narrow creek. On the far side, the path widened, and a cluster of nearly identical one-story stone homes stood along both sides.

Each house had a narrow wood door in the middle front, with two small windows on either side. The homes weren't dilapidated—just basic, small, and jammed together.

Two old women stood and curtsied. Young children stared for a moment and then ran away.

"It's so unlike Camden House or even New Plymouth."

"This is one of the nicer helot villages I've seen. About ten years ago Father ran power and water to it from the mansion."

"How often do you come here?"

"Um … that was the last time."

A gasp turned Rachel around. Anna and Naomi stood a few yards back holding a covered basket between them. The smells of bread, meats, and baked goods drifted to Rachel's nose.

"What's this?" Lucas asked sternly.

Rachel smiled. "It smells like dinner."

Lucas frowned, walked to the two girls, and pulled back the cover. "Except servants aren't allowed to remove food from the house."

Chapter 18

Devon system, Planet Exeter

Rachel stepped close to Lucas. "But today is a celebration of your mother's life, and a loving mother would want children and families to be fed. Right?" She gave him a hard stare.

Lucas cast a guilty grin. "Yes, of course."

Relieved, Rachel pulled the cloth back over the food. She might not be a Seeker, but she often felt like their protector. Her gaze shifted between the two women. "Is the village your home?"

"Oh, no," Anna replied. "We both live in the mansion, but our parents and family live here."

"May we go along with you?" Rachel looked to the nearby homes. "I'd love to meet your family."

Anna's eyes flared wide and she glanced between Rachel and Lucas.

After a moment, Naomi spoke. "Of course, Lady Rachel. I'd like that very much."

"So, I'm a lady now?" Rachel grinned.

"It's easier and safer than calling you Daughter of Earth." Naomi turned and pointed toward the village. "Our families live next to each other just ahead."

Rachel and Lucas followed them across the bridge. Several children had returned to the area but scattered as the four approached.

The small stone homes matched in nearly every detail, but Rachel's eyes fixed on the front door of the house Naomi approached. The top half bore a carved cross and globe similar to the one she'd seen in the chapel. The bottom half displayed an elaborate carving of what could've been a thanksgiving feast. Her eyes paused on the bearded man at the center. Except for the main door of the mansion, she had seen nothing like it.

"This is where I grew up. My parents and grandmother still live here." Naomi turned a diamond-shaped wood knob and, with Anna, crossed the threshold amid excited conversation.

Rachel followed, fiddling with the fancy knob as she passed.

Lucas entered behind her.

All conversation stopped.

A man about the age of Rachel's father stepped forward. "Lord Lucas, you have my sympathy on the loss of your mother. I welcome you and your friend to my home."

"Thank you. Please pay me no mind." He touched Rachel's arm. "This is Miss Rachel. I was showing her the grounds, and Naomi kindly invited us in."

A murmur arose in the room, and Rachel heard several whisper her name. Their host fixed his eyes on her. "My name is Joshua. Naomi is my daughter. She's already told me much about you. You are welcome in this place. Please, share a meal with us."

Shouts and claps of agreement erupted from all around.

"Uh, no thank you. That isn't necessary." Rachel's protestations went unheard among the cheers. When quiet returned, she relented. "I'd love to."

Joshua introduced her to siblings, aunts, and uncles, and then it continued as neighbors joined them inside the home. Soon Rachel remembered only Joshua's name.

Joshua walked over and pulled out two chairs next to a simple but well-crafted wood table. "Please, Lord Lucas and Miss Rachel, be seated here." He looked around the crowded room. "Please, everyone sit, if you can find a chair, and be comfortable."

One seat at the table remained empty. Naomi entered from another room holding the arm of an old woman.

"This is my grandmother, Ruth." Naomi helped her to the empty seat across from Rachel.

The old woman smiled, reached out, and touched Rachel's hand. "I thank the God of Earth for allowing me to live long enough to see you."

Rachel felt her face flush.

The others stared but said nothing.

All the attention made Rachel regret coming into the home. In desperation she spoke. "It's taken me a long time to explore. Well, I did need to recover from the crash and then there was the battle and all that, but now I really want to learn more about all of you, this village, and Exeter." She hoped that would spur conversation, but no one spoke, so she turned to Lucas. "I'm glad you've made me a guest in your home, but I feel like I have so much to learn about ....."

Did they know where she was from? Did they know Anna and Naomi called her Daughter of Earth? Probably, but she needed to be careful.

"Ah, there's so much to learn about this world."

"We have an excellent library at the house." Lucas leaned back in the chair. "With a palmcomp you could connect to others and learn anything you wanted to know."

"That's great." Rachel looked around. "But some things aren't written in books."

Lucas frowned. "Such as?"

She struggled to find an illustrative example that wouldn't reveal much about her.

"Uh, doors. Most at the mansion are just flat panels with no knobs, but this home has such a fancy, elaborately carved door." Rachel pointed to the entrance. "The main door of the mansion is very similar. Why is that?" *Probably not the best example, but common and conversational.*

"My father carved both the mansion door and this one." Joshua cast a sad smile.

Rachel glanced at the door. "Such a skilled carver. The mansion door must've cost a fortune."

Joshua turned his gaze to the door, but said nothing.

"Lord Baldwin allowed my grandfather to cut down the tree used to make that door." Naomi set bread on the table. "That was his payment."

"*Naomi,*" Joshua barked.

"At the time, these homes had no power," Naomi continued. "That's why it has a knob."

"Enough, Naomi!" Joshua slammed his fist on the table. "Don't insult guests in my house."

"Yes, Father." She hurried back to the kitchen.

Who knew that doors and knobs could be so controversial? Apparently, everyone in the room but me. No more questions.

Naomi and her mother entered carrying trays of food.

Rachel sighed, relieved that attention had been diverted from her.

The meal consisted mainly of leftovers from the mansion with some breads, soup, and a bowl filled with a brown root plant. Rachel asked about the other foods.

Joshua pointed to the bowl. "The tanger and some of the wheat grew on plots near the village."

Had she eaten food meant for them and their children? Rachel nibbled at the food on her plate through the rest of the meal, and took no more. "This is all very good, but I think I've had enough." She smiled and set down her spoon.

After the meal, when Rachel stood ready to leave, Lucas asked Naomi to follow. The three walked together across the simple bridge that spanned the creek. When on the other side, Lucas said, "I've known you all my life Naomi, and only now do I see the resentment that must've been building for years. However, I'm not your enemy."

"This resentment, as you call it, is a desire for freedom, nothing more. It's been growing in many of us for years, but before there existed little hope of change." She smiled at Rachel. "Now there is real hope."

Rachel cringed.

Lucas took a deep breath and let it out. "I hope for change also, but you and all other Seekers need to be careful with what you say."

"We will be careful—until the time for freedom."

"When will that be?" Lucas held up his palms.

"Lady Rachel will know."

"Me? I don't know."

"I doubt all of you can be that careful, that long." Lucas shook his head. "Someone will say or do something, and Nightwatch will descend upon us all. And you talk of freedom as if you're a slave. You're not. You're free."

"Free to leave this place?"

Lucas remained silent for a moment. "Well, no, but you're paid."

"Not much. A tree or a pittance." Naomi scowled. "We're serfs bound in service to the Baldwin family." Without another word, Naomi curtsied to Rachel, turned, and hurried away.

"Are you still mad at Naomi for taking food from the mansion?" Rachel asked as she and Lucas walked back along the path.

"No. I told Father about it years ago, and he's done nothing." Lucas shrugged. "I see now that the food is a help to them." They walked awhile in silence, and then Lucas continued. "I'm growing more fearful for Naomi—for all of them and us also. If events get out of hand, Nightwatch and Prince Draven will pounce."

"Your world is really messed up." Rachel shook her head. "People are oppressed, there's a war that never ends, and some are really rich while others are very poor."

"Yes, there are real problems." Lucas nodded. "So Earth has overcome these issues? People aren't oppressed, and there's no war, and everyone has what they need?"

Rachel searched his face for sarcasm but found none. "No, Earth has plenty of problems."

"Then perhaps it's the human condition that leads to such problems, not the location."

She pondered his statement as they continued toward the mansion. Lucas might be right, Rachel concluded, but she felt a growing allegiance with the Seekers.

* * *

Four days later, Farold sat at his desk in the operations center and stared at his palmcomp, reading and rereading three messages that had arrived during the night.

In the last few days, he had come to hope that he'd won a victory. Not against the Valac, but at least a symbolic one against the powers of Terra. He dared to hope it might stop Nightwatch's attempts to kill his family and give him time to develop a long-range plan and a proposal to set before the king and Privy Council. But now hope had faded.

Again, he gazed at the three messages. The first advised that his eldest son, Victor had been presented to King Aelfric, promoted to major, and in a few weeks would return home to assist with the rebuilding of the planetary defense forces. Any father should be proud.

Delete.

The second message told Farold that elements of the Pegasus and Taurus fleets would arrive at Devon tomorrow to assist with security and defense. Normally, this would please him, but now it felt less like a protective embrace and more like the king asserting authority over a wayward system.

Delete.

Had all the plots and intrigue stirred up irrational thoughts? He might have dismissed it all as such except that the last message, from Aelfric, seemed to confirm the worst.

Save.

Farold shut the palmcomp off and left his office. Later, after returning home, he still pondered the messages. Usually, he maintained a brisk pace, but today he found himself ambling along, deep in thought. He sighed as he approached the dining room door, not quite ready to smile and make small talk.

The new butler snapped to attention as Farold entered. Conversation continued as friends, family, and guests moved to their places. Farold joined everyone at the table but remained standing. When they all sat, he put on his best smile. "My family and I shall be leaving soon. We have received a royal invitation from King Aelfric."

Chapter 19

Devon system, Planet Exeter

Farold struggled to maintain a pleased expression as he clapped softly at his own news of the royal invitation. His gaze drifted over the wide-eyed enthusiasm of extended family, still here after the funeral.

These untitled relatives gained wealth and power by their relationship to his branch of the family. Now they would cling all the tighter, hoping that by close association they might further increase their stature.

While keeping a smile on his face, Farold frowned inwardly, knowing how tenuous his position was, and how quickly most of those assembled would desert him if the king or Nightwatch accused him of treason.

Farold reached for his glass. The traditional toast to the king concluded with, "May he lead us to ever greater victories over the Valac," but Farold didn't want to say that. He raised the glass as the room fell silent. "To King Aelfric."

Glasses hung in mid-air, awaiting the end of the toast.

Tybalt jumped to his feet. "King Aelfric."

The room thundered with the king's name.

*   *   *

In the hallway after dinner, Rachel strolled alongside Lucas. With a smile she took his arm. "I'm getting to know you better."

"How so?"

"When you heard of the invitation from King Aelfric you smiled, but you weren't happy."

Lucas chuckled. "I'm pleased you're getting to know me better."

"Now *that's* a real smile," she grinned. "Do you have to visit the king?"

"A royal invitation is more like a summons than a simple request. You might have a splendid time—but go you must."

The now-familiar shimmer of light heralded Sarah's appearance. "Lord Baldwin requires the presence of both of you at his office in fifteen minutes."

Lucas turned to Rachel. "Another form of mandatory invitation. Father might have good news, but whatever it is, we must comply with the summons. You go ahead; I've got something I must do first."

Rachel continued around the corner, but hearing a thud and a curse from Lucas, she turned back to investigate. As she rounded the corner, she spotted Lucas on the floor. "Are you okay?"

"Yes," he grunted.

"Can I help?"

"Pass me my leg, please." He pointed to his prosthetic leg just out of reach.

She did. "What happened?"

For several moments he said nothing as he worked to reattach the limb. Then he sighed. "As my limbs grow, they constantly itch. I removed the leg to scratch the spot and fell."

"So the thing you had to do so urgently was scratch?" Rachel stifled a grin. "Next time just ask me to help you."

"I don't like you seeing me as an invalid."

"I see you as a soldier recovering from battlefield wounds. It doesn't bother me to see you without your limbs."

He cast a skeptical glance her way.

"Okay, maybe it bothers me a bit. I'm fine with it, though. I'm glad they'll grow back, but the thought of it is still weird."

"For me, it's strange that yours don't." He stood and rolled down his pant leg. "If you break a leg or arm, would the bone grow back?"

"Yes, of course it would."

"But limbs don't?" He shook his head. "Weird."

Lucas offered her his arm, and together they continued on toward Farold's office.

"Tell me about your older brother." Rachel spotted fresh tension on his face. "I shouldn't be nosy. I'm sorry."

Lucas took a deep breath. "No, it's okay. What do you want to know?"

"Well, I'm pretty sure he's your half-brother, and I've noticed you don't like being compared to him."

"Yes he is my half-brother and probably most younger brothers don't like being compared, but beyond that we've never been close. I suspect he doesn't even like me."

"Why would you say that?"

Lucas remained silent as they started up the stairs. "Father's first marriage was arranged by his parents. Such marriages are common among the nobility, and I don't think they ever loved each other. When she died in a dart accident, father had already come into his inheritance. So he married the woman he had always loved—my mother."

"So he didn't marry your mother for money?"

"There's great pressure on us, the nobility, to marry at, or above, our station in life. My mother was a teacher at the local school."

Rachel shook her head, not understanding.

"My mother is … was a commoner before she married father."

"Shocking." Rachel slapped a hand over her heart.

"You jest, but many scorned my father when he married her."

"Frankly, I'm starting to like your dad."

They reached the top of the stairs and continued along the hall toward the office.

Katherine strode down the hall from the other direction. Her gaze fixed on Lucas and Rachel's intertwined arms, and she smiled. "Has cupid's arrow struck?"

Lucas's face flushed. "We're friends."

Rachel felt her face warm and tried to casually withdraw her arm, but Lucas held firm.

Katherine grinned and nodded. "What does Father want?"

Lucas shrugged, released Rachel's arm, and put his bracelet to the door. "Let's go in and find out."

When they all sat down in the office, Farold leaned back in his chair. "King Aelfric hasn't just invited the Baldwin family to Novam Terram. He also wants to meet Miss Rachel Harper."

"Me?" Rachel gasped. "The king wants to meet me?"

"I'm certain Prince Draven has kept the king apprised of your presence here," Farold said.

"That's not good." Rachel felt nauseated.

Farold fixed his eyes on her, and his brow furrowed. "Almost certainly it's not."

"I'm sorry I've caused you all this trouble." Rachel's head slumped and she wiped her eyes. "It's my fault you're in danger, my fault this world was attacked, and my fault Lady Charlotte is dead. Maybe it would've been better if the Aux had just killed me."

"I did at one time blame you, but I no longer do." Farold stood and walked around the desk to Rachel. "I don't know why the Aux snatched you from Earth, but whatever the reason, you are innocent. Indeed, the Aux kidnapped you and brought you here. They are the villains."

He pulled a handkerchief from his jacket pocket and handed it to her.

"I suspect the Aux acted on behalf of the Mage," Lucas added.

Farold stepped to Lucas and placed a hand on his shoulder. "I agree. Furthermore, you did right in helping Rachel." He moved to Katherine and squeezed her hand.

"And you did right by bringing her here." He returned to his seat behind the desk. "I've never told anyone about this, not even your mother." For several moments, he said nothing. "I've known of Earth's existence and that there had been no attack—"

"You *knew?*" Lucas shook his head. "When? How?"

"I've known for nearly ten years." Farold frowned. "After an evening of much drinking, King Aelfric revealed the truth with me. We drank so much that night that I have often wondered if he even remembers telling me."

"The helots, Seekers, spoke the truth." Lucas grinned. "That's why you've turned a blind eye to the stealing of food from the kitchen."

Farold nodded. "I should have done more."

Rachel wiped her eyes. "After you learned the truth, that's when you installed power to the village."

"Yes." Farold seemed to stare into the distance for several moments. "From Alton we learned that the crown has turned against us. While we're on Novam Terram, we must remain united, vigilant, and cautious.

"Still, I'm a marquis of the Kingdom of Europa, and I want to stand before my peers and state my case." Then, in a softer voice, he added, "But if I do, it will put you three in even greater danger."

"Since this began, we've been in great danger." Lucas stood. "But we don't want a revolution. Rachel wants to go home, and the Valac want peace. Who could argue with that?"

For a moment, no one moved or said anything. Then Rachel reached into her bodice and retrieved the crystal Tybalt had hidden with her onboard the *Argonaut*. "Perhaps this will help."

She hesitated, recalling that the crystal held images of her naked. She rolled it from her hand to Farold's, her best chance of survival.

"You'll need my help." Katherine stood. "Two people are needed to unlock the crystal."

* * *

After everyone left Farold placed his office into secure mode and viewed the contents of the crystal, cringing at both the torture and humiliation Rachel had endured. It would take time to analyze and translate all the information, but even a quick perusal destroyed the lie of history as taught in all the kingdoms of Terra.

Farold rolled the crystal between his fingers. Perhaps they would survive—and have the opportunity of revenge against the royal family. He copied the contents of the crystal.

The palmcomp dinged with an incoming message. Farold tapped the display and a holo image of Brian, the journalist, appeared in the center of the room.

"Has everything been prepared?" Farold asked.

"Yes, Admiral. They're ready for release."

"I'm leaving tomorrow for Novam Terram. Begin the release tonight, but before then, we need to meet."

"Yes, Admiral." Brian's face flushed. "I know this isn't appropriate but … well, as I've learned more these last few days, my opinion on many things has changed—including my opinion about you. I hope this works. May the God of Earth be with you."

Chapter 20

Enroute Novam Terram

As the Baldwin family dart rose into the blue sky, Rachel sat in the same seat and stared out the same window that she had before the Last Night ceremony. The engines roared louder as the sky darkened from pastel blue to black, and thousands of stars appeared. "I don't think I'll ever get use to this."

Lucas, sitting across from her, leaned forward and looked out. "That's nice, but take a look out the starboard side." He stood and gestured for her to follow.

Rachel stepped past Katherine, who wore a silver vid headset and swayed to unheard tunes, and followed Lucas to the other side of the craft.

"That's Exeter's northern hemisphere." Lucas pointed out the window.

Large blue oceans surrounded continents of green and brown. In the far north, a white polar cap topped it off, and billowy white clouds accented the globe.

"Your world is very beautiful."

They both returned to their original seats, and Lucas pointed again. "That's the family yacht, *Veritas*."

All Rachel could see was a bright white star. "That dot?"

Lucas grinned. "It'll grow as we get close."

"Does the name mean anything?"

"It means truth."

Another Lingua Terra word to remember. Rachel continued to stare out the window. Soon the dot stretched into a long silver starship. A hatch slid open on the *Veritas*, and the dart flew in and settled to the deck with a clank and clang. A few minutes later, the ramp at the rear of the dart lowered to the *Veritas* deck. Farold stepped out with Lucas one step behind. Katherine and Rachel followed.

About fifty men in uniform stood at attention in a semi-circle near the ramp.

A silver-haired officer stepped forward and saluted Farold. "Welcome back to the *Veritas*, Lord Baldwin. When do you wish to set sail?"

"Thank you, Captain." Farold shook his hand. "I'm ready when you are."

"Then I'll get back to the bridge, sir. We'll get you to King Aelfric as quickly as possible." He saluted and left.

Rachel leaned close to Katherine. "Should we get our luggage off before the dart leaves?"

"The dart stays." Katherine pointed to the new butler, Farold's former valet, alongside Anna and Naomi at the back of the crowd. "They'll take care of the luggage."

The plight of the Seekers continued to trouble Rachel. It was one thing to voluntarily serve someone else. Firefighters, police, nurses, and military often did, but they were much better paid and had a choice. Should she go back and get her own luggage?

She decided to wait before causing a commotion. The time would come.

As they stepped away from the dart, Rachel noticed another ship. "Is that the *Lady Katherine*?" She pointed to a large dart tied down at the far end of the bay.

Katherine cast a big smile. "The repairs were made, so I convinced Father to bring her along. I can't wait to use it."

Led by a steward clothed in the plain tunic of a Seeker, the four exited the bay and headed down a long passageway.

Glancing back, Rachel estimated the corridor stretched fifty yards behind them and nearly a hundred ahead. "How big is this yacht?"

"Just over 800 feet from bow to stern." Lucas slowed and walked alongside Rachel. "*Veritas* is a decommissioned marine assault vessel. The family bought it from the crown as scrap and refurbished it. It's still armed and has performed missions as a privateer."

Something clanked behind her, and Rachel again looked back. Burdened with luggage, the household staff followed far behind.

"This way." Lucas took Rachel's arm. "Our rooms are on the starboard side near the bow."

The group turned down another passageway and then another. The steward unlocked a door as a weird, but now familiar feeling swept through Rachel.

The *Veritas* had jumped into a Mage Tunnel toward Novam Terram.

Lucas stumbled.

Rachel grabbed his arm. "Those prosthetic limbs can be clumsy."

Rachel stood to the side impatiently waiting while the other were shown to their rooms. Finally the steward nodded to her and unlocked a door.

The compartment appeared larger than those on the *Lady Katherine* and even more lavish. A floor-to-ceiling window, framed in red curtains, allowed the kaleidoscope of Mage Tunnel colors to swirl across the room. Several thick rugs covered its hardwood floors. Paintings adorned each wall, and she recognized one that depicted the gardens at Camden House.

With her arms spread wide, she dropped backward onto the large bed. As she lay there, she recalled the question she had asked herself that first day on the *Lady Katherine*: *How rich do you have to be to own your own cruise ship?* She now knew the answer—wealthy beyond anything on Earth.

The door chimed, and Katherine entered, followed by a heavily burdened Anna.

"Dinner's in one hour." Katherine stepped out of Anna's path. "Lucas says there'll be a surprise then." She shook her head. "Usually, when we're on the *Veritas* we have family and friends along, and we dance after dinner. I'm not dancing with my father or brother."

Rachel sat cross-legged on the bed. "There's the crew."

Katherine's shoulders slumped. "I might be watching vids for the next five days."

"I'd like to see what Lucas has planned, but I'd really like you to be there too."

Katherine sighed heavily. "Okay, if you promise to save me from anyone who wants to dance."

*　*　*

Farold and Lucas were already in the dining room when Rachel and Katherine strolled in. Only one table, surrounded by six chairs, stood in a room that might have held a hundred.

As they sat around the table, the butler entered carrying a silver tray.

"What's your surprise, brother?" Katherine asked.

Lucas pulled a palmcomp from his pocket and tapped the screen.

After a momentary shimmer, people appeared as if by magic. Couples danced, while others appeared to chat along the sides. At the far end of the room a quartet played soft music.

"This is wonderful." Rachel's gaze swept the room. "Is it a holoview projection?"

Lucas nodded and smiled.

Other servants entered with more trays as the butler filled glasses with wine.

"*That's* your surprise?" Katherine rolled her eyes. "I've seen better."

"No, that's not my surprise."

Farold turned to Lucas. "Hold the dancing until after dinner."

Lucas tapped the screen again, and the dancers disappeared.

A moment later, Tybalt strolled into the compartment in full dress uniform. "Sorry I'm late."

Farold smiled. "I didn't know you were aboard."

Lucas leaned close to his sister. "That's the surprise."

Tybalt sat across from Rachel. "My platoon has been assigned to protect your family."

"Shall I save you from him?" Rachel whispered to Katherine.

"No." Katherine flushed. "I think I can handle him myself."

Farold stared at Katherine and Lucas. Then he leaned back in his chair with a frown. "I wonder how that happened."

After dinner, Lucas brought the dancers back and turned to Rachel. "May I have the first dance?"

"You might regret that request." Rachel felt her face warm. "I'm not a good dancer."

"This is the perfect place to learn." Lucas held out his hand.

On the dance floor, Rachel placed her hands as Tybalt had shown her. Careful to follow Lucas's lead, she twirled with him around the floor. Rachel concentrated on not stepping on Lucas's feet and still managed to enjoy his embrace.

He was so different from the immature, but over-sexed, boys she'd known back in Seattle. Lucas had character and courage beyond his years. For a moment she imagined life on Devon with Lucas.

As they spun about, Tybalt and Katherine came into view, dancing nearby. Katherine loved Tybalt, but would Farold allow his daughter to marry beneath her rank? Katherine didn't seem to think it possible.

Distracted, Rachel stumbled into a holographic dancing couple, fluttering the image for a moment.

Lucas grinned. "When I was young, I would run through them." He plunged an arm into a nearby couple, and they fluttered and distorted.

Rachel smiled but said nothing. The feeling that now brewed within her suffered from the same problem Katherine had with Tybalt. According to the class structure of these worlds, the man who held her in his arms was a noble, and in these worlds, she was a commoner. Anything beyond dinner and a dance would be impossible.

"Is something bothering you?" Lucas asked.

She shook her head. "This is lovely."

Lucas leaned close as he raised an eyebrow.

"Aren't you worried about what'll happen when we get to Novam Terram?"

Lucas smiled. "Not tonight."

*   *   *

Talking, laughing, eating, and dancing filled the days and much of the night until they arrived in orbit over the capital planet.

"Good morning."

Rachel struggled to open her eyes. "Sarah? What time is it?"

"Five in the morning, ship time, and eight in the evening, capital time."

She moaned and pulled the blankets over her head. "I'm going to have awful jetlag. Go away."

"The *Veritas* is in orbit over Novam Terram. Lord Baldwin requires all the royal guests to wake and be ready for departure in one hour."

"Well, go wake Katherine or Lucas."

"I am."

A moment later, Rachel peeked from the covers. Sarah stood smiling nearby. "Anna has arrived. Shall I let her in?"

Rachel sighed in surrender and rolled to a sitting position. "If you must."

Sarah disappeared into a shower of flickers.

Anna entered. "Good morning, Lady Rachel. I'll draw you a bath." She dashed through a side door and returned a few moments later holding up a deep purple dress for approval. "Will this be the day freedom arrives?"

Rachel pulled the hair back from her face. "Not if I have to make it happen."

After breakfast, the royal guests boarded the family dart. Rachel stared out the familiar window as the craft launched into space. She had followed Lucas's example and tucked her fears away, in a back corner of her mind, and now they stormed into her consciousness.

The Aux wanted to torture her for some unknown reason, and the powers of this kingdom wanted her dead in order to hide the truth that Earth existed. At least she understood that reason, but had it been a good idea to walk into the king's grasp?

They orbited the blue-and-green world of Novam Terram and then dipped into the atmosphere, descended through blue skies, across twilight, into the evening darkness. City lights dotted the surface like jewels of every color spread across a velvet surface. As they neared, towers of light rose into the sky, and darts, like long lines of fireflies, wove through the city.

Their craft made a long sweeping turn, and Lucas pointed. "There's the palace. We'll land on one of the towers."

Darkness obscured what must've been a huge structure. Rachel wished they'd arrived during the day. Darkness might lend beauty, but it also lent mystery and made everything more foreboding. She pointed to a long line of lights that looked almost like a runway. "What's that?"

"The Avenue of Heroes. We'll see it in daylight soon."

The dart flew above one of the towers, descended slowly, and, with a slight thud, came to rest. Moments later, the ramp slid down revealing a crowd of hundreds.

And there, at the bottom waiting to greet them, stood a smiling Prince Draven.

Chapter 21

Novam Terram

Hundreds of cheering, clapping people pressed close to the line of royal guards as Farold stepped off the ramp and bowed to Prince Draven.

"Welcome to Novam Terram, Lord Admiral Baldwin." Prince Draven held out his hand. "I've seen so much of you and your brave family these last few days."

With a firm grip, Farold grasped the hand of the prince. "Vids? I don't pay them much attention." He squeezed. "But I'm glad you were able to watch."

Prince Draven grimaced and tried to withdraw his hand.

Farold clasped the prince's hand with both of his and smiled. "Lady Charlotte would've loved the chance to be here." Still smiling he pressed even harder, hoping to break a royal bone or two.

"It's regrettable that she isn't with you." The prince paled.

"Perhaps I'll get a chance to talk with you about her sometime. She was a most interesting woman, and I loved her very much."

"Love." Prince Draven winced. "Yes, I too feel some pain regarding her death. Shall we postpone such uncomfortable matters and proceed to the palace?"

"Yes. I look forward to talking again, perhaps just the two of us alone." Farold whispered and released Draven's hand. But he vowed to find the right time and place to kill the little prince.

With a trembling hand and a supressed groan, the prince stepped back.

* * *

A few feet behind, Lucas watched the greeting and handshake with Prince Draven. How could his father be so calm and polite? Upon the command of Prince Draven his father's wife, the mother of his two youngest children—Lucas's mother, had been murdered. The royal villain had ordered the whole family killed. Anger boiled within Lucas. If his father couldn't, or wouldn't do it, Lucas would find a way to kill Prince Draven.

Prince Draven stepped away with a pained look. Had his father said something? Lucas hoped so.

* * *

Seeing Prince Draven at the bottom of the ramp, Rachel shuddered. The man responsible for the murder of Lady Charlotte and the attempts on Katherine's, Naomi's, and her life now talked politely with Farold. How could Farold do that? A combination of fear and disgust swirled inside of Rachel at the mere sight of Draven.

The two men released their handshake, and Draven backed away several steps with a pained expression on his face. Then he turned and strode toward large metal doors. The guards cleared a path, and the entourage followed.

The guards opened twenty-foot-high steel doors, and Draven led them within. Rachel stepped through, looked over the edge, and grabbed the rail tight. They had walked onto a sky-bridge a hundred feet above sculpted gardens, trees, and ponds.

In the evening darkness, many of the trees glowed, some by tiny lights, while others simply gleamed from within. Stones along the paths below cast the soft colors of a rainbow. Even the ponds reflected an unreal blue glow.

The sky-bridge curved toward a palace on a nearby hill. All the lights of the garden cast their radiance to the five-story granite-and-marble structure, lending it a magical quality.

Regaining her composure, Rachel caught up with Katherine. "Are we staying here?"

"Of course," Katherine replied.

"Wow." Rachel slowed her pace and leaned over the rail to take in more of the view. Off to one side, a small waterfall fed a pond filled with fish of every color. A nearby footbridge led to a small island with a gazebo. She stood straight, casting a wider gaze. A stone wall surrounded the palace and gardens. Standing still, she marveled at the display of beauty, wealth, and power.

"Rachel?" Lucas touched her arm. "The others have gone inside."

"Oh." She walked with him to the end of the sky-bridge where two footmen, dressed in matching dark suits, held large wooden doors open. Despite their fine clothes, Rachel wondered if they were Seekers.

Just beyond the entrance hung a larger-than-life portrait of a man in a purple cape with gray beard and hair. Now alone in the hall, Rachel paused. "Was that a painting of the king?"

"Yes." Lucas grinned. "Every child knows that's the official portrait of the king."

She thumped him on the arm. "I know what the president looks like."

"The what?"

"Exactly." She walked ahead, but the many doors and perpendicular hallways left her confused. She had no idea where to go, so Rachel stopped and waited.

Lucas strolled toward her. "Lost, are you?"

"No." She smirked. "Just waiting for the invalid."

He grinned and pointed. "The guest apartments are this way."

The two caught up with the others as a male servant escorted Farold to his room and gave Lucas the room next door. Katherine had the room across from him, and then the servant opened the next door for Rachel.

Glad that everyone was nearby, she relaxed and followed the servant into her room. Only when she stood inside did she realize the scale of the space. She strolled through the entryway into a living room, complete with a couch, chairs, and tables.

The servant opened the door to the bedroom. "Will this do, Miss Rachel?"

"Uh, yes … sure, of course."

Lucas had called this an apartment, but these rooms, nearly the size of her home on Earth, seemed more like a luxury suite at a grand hotel. She looked around a corner. There were lots of places for an assassin to hide.

The servant pulled a palmcomp from his belt. "The king desires that you have access to the common spaces of the palace. If you give me your bracelet, I'll make the changes.

The servant upgraded the device and left. Rachel inspected the other rooms. All of them had wood floors with plush area rugs. Paintings adorned walls, and heavy curtains framed expansive windows. She certainly detected a theme among the rich of Europa. She wondered if all the kingdoms of Terra were similar.

As she strolled back, Sarah blinked into the middle of the living room. "King Aelfric summons—"

"What?" Rachel stumbled back a few steps. "How did you get here?"

"I follow the Baldwin family." Sarah seemed to smile. "King Aelfric summons you and Lord Baldwin to the privy council chamber."

"Huh? Now? Uh, get Lord Baldwin—"

"He awaits you in the corridor." Sarah disappeared.

Rachel exhaled and joined Farold in the hall. "Why do you think he wants to talk with just us?"

"Well, you *are* the woman from Earth." Farold gestured down the hallway, and they walked side-by-side. "Also, I'm the noble who offered you protection."

"I meant right now, just minutes after we arrive."

"Oh, that." Farold frowned. "The king wants to intimidate us."

"He's rich and powerful. I get it."

"I've been a loyal servant of the king for many years. I've even called him a friend." Farold shrugged. "But, like a viper, if you aren't careful, he can take your life in flash."

Rachel shuddered. "Okay, I'm intimidated."

"Good." Farold stopped and locked eyes with her. "Do you trust me?"

She nodded.

"Then say little while we are with him, and I'll try to save all of our lives."

They continued down to the hall to a door with two soldiers posted outside. The guards opened the door. Farold entered first, and Rachel followed.

She stopped just inside to allow her eyes time to adjust. On a platform, a step up from the main floor, sat a tall, finely carved, wood chair. *A throne?* A window behind it cast the throne in an almost spiritual glow. In front of it, on the main floor of the chamber, stood a large wood table.

Prince Draven strode into the room.

Farold bowed, and Rachel curtsied.

Prince Draven grunted and walked to the far end of the table.

Moments later, King Aelfric entered through a side door on the platform and settled into the throne.

Prince Draven and Farold bowed. The king seemed to stare at Rachel as she curtsied.

"Be seated." The king waved his arm. "Let's get this over with."

Legs trembling, Rachel hurried to a seat at the far end of the table. Farold sat on her left in the middle and stared straight ahead at King Aelfric. Across from her sat Draven, who seemed to stare at his father. With slow hesitation, Rachel cast her gaze to the king.

"So you're the one who has caused all these problems."

"Uh …."

"I didn't ask you anything." He turned to Farold. "I've heard much about you lately. All the vid outlets carried word of your epic battle to save the Devon system. The vids and pictures of you, Lucas, and an unidentified woman," he glanced at Rachel, "surrounded by Valac outside of your manor house. Very compelling. How did you survive?"

Rachel's heart pounded. Would Farold tell King Aelfric how she had communicated with the Valac? That they wanted peace?

Farold started to answer, but the king continued.

"I wanted to share a final meal with you and then have you executed, but how can I kill a hero of the kingdom? I may have to give you a medal." The king massaged his temple. "I only recently became aware of the Earth girl, and my son's attempts to kill her and those around her. Instead of using the finesse necessary to be an effective leader, Draven prefers being a brute." King Aelfric glared at his son. "Even so, he is often ineffective."

Draven jumped to his feet. "Father, I did what the Mage—"

"*Silence!*" The king slammed his fist on the arm of the chair. "Sit down."

Draven face paled. He sat.

The king spoke to Farold in a softer tone. "I regret the death of Charlotte. I had come to appreciate her. I also regret the recent lack of military support for Devon. I would have handled both situations differently."

"I am pleased to hear that, Your Highness," Farold said.

"Perhaps if you had involved me earlier, we might've reached a more amicable arrangement." King Aelfric stroked his beard. "But that now seems unlikely. As I said, I brought you and your family here for execution, but you're a master of strategy and used the journalists and vids well. So, I've decided to use that cunning.

"Within two days, I require a plan to eliminate the Earth girl and the helots that now preach her treason. This must be done in a quiet, expedient and thorough way. If it isn't done, I will turn you and your children over to Prince Draven and Nightwatch for execution."

Chapter 22

Novam Terram

Rachel shuddered, and bile rose in her throat. Had the king just ordered her execution? Her eyes darted from a scowling King Aelfric to a grinning Prince Draven.

The king stood. "I will meet with you again in forty-eight hours."

Dizzy with fear, Rachel struggled to stand as Farold and Draven bowed.

King Aelfric strode from the room.

She knew that Prince Draven wanted her dead, but would Farold carry out the order to save his own life? Even if his life wasn't in peril, the lives of Lucas and Katherine were. Would Farold kill her to save his children? She stumbled out the door trying to get away.

Prince Draven exited right behind her. "Are you all right?" His voice dripped with sincerity. "Shall I call a doctor?"

Rachel fell against the wall and held out her arms to block his approach. "No!"

"I'll see to her, Your Highness." Farold stepped close to the prince.

Rachel ran from them both. She turned down one hall and then another and quickly got lost in the massive palace. It didn't matter. She just wanted to be left alone.

With a glance over her shoulder, she confirmed no one had followed her. A relieved sigh escaped her lips as she stumbled forward, head down, with one hand against the wall.

Something whooshed just ahead, and she looked up. Large double-doors stood open. She glanced at her bracelet; apparently it had opened the door. She hurried into the room, and the doors closed.

Rachel ignored the opulent couches, chairs, and tables that dotted the drawing chamber as she walked toward one of the large windows that overlooked the gardens. This room seemed a good place to hide and think, so she retreated to a corner, collapsed into a chair and stared into the starless night.

Gradually worry pushed to the forefront of her mind. Would Farold really kill her? She doubted it, but she couldn't exclude the possibility. Even if Farold didn't murder her, she would likely die here.

Please, God, help me, keep my friends safe, and show me a way back to Earth.

The door slid open, and Anna stepped in, followed by Naomi.

"I didn't call for you." Rachel turned away and stared out the window into darkness. "How did you find me?"

"Your bracelet gives your location." Anna stepped forward. "Lord Baldwin and Sir Lucas are waiting outside."

"King Aelfric wants me dead. Have they come to carry out the order?"

"No." Anna stepped closer. "I would never partici-pate in you being harmed."

Naomi shook her head "I wouldn't either. All my life, I've been forced to bow and submit to people who don't deserve it." Naomi curtsied. "If you wish to flee the pal-ace right now, I'll help you."

Anna nodded. "But Lord Baldwin and Sir Lucas aren't here to harm. They're worried about you."

The knot of anxiety in her stomach relaxed a bit. Rachel sighed. "Okay, but I'm staying put. Tell them if they want to talk, they need to come here."

As soon as he and Lucas reached the room, Farold turned to Anna and Naomi. "Use Sarah to find Kather-ine and bring her here."

The two servants curtsied and hurried from the room.

Farold sat at a table away from the windows and placed a silver cylinder about the size of a soda can on the table. He gestured to Rachel. "Please join us here. This device will give us privacy while it's green." He tapped it.

The device hummed, turned red, and then faded to green.

Lucas sat beside him, and Rachel followed.

"What's going on, Father?"

"King Aelfric wants me to orchestrate the murder of Rachel and the helots that know her as the Daughter of Earth."

"Why you?" Lucas leaned in.

"I suspect he wants me to prove my loyalty." Farold shook his head. "It will also give King Aelfric power over the situation."

Rachel didn't understand, and it must've shown on her face.

"If I murder you and kill a few hundred helots, in the way the king commands, and anyone finds out about it, I will appear to be the guilty one. The king's hands are clean. Furthermore, the king can use his knowledge of your murder as a means to keep me in my place."

Lucas shook his head. "What can we do?"

The ball flashed red, and then it returned to green.

"Did you forget to charge the Null Space?" Lucas asked

"I didn't plan on using it this soon." Farold grasped the cylinder. "I'm going to find Katherine, recharge it, and get some sleep. We have two days to come up with a proposal. We'll meet again tomorrow and hopefully develop a plan."

*   *   *

Unable to sleep, Katherine strolled from the palace into the gardens. Learning about Earth had changed her. As a child, she had sometimes imagined discovering Earth still full of vibrant life.

It had always made her happy, but since the day of the battle—the day of her mother's death—a cold lump of numbness gnawed at her. She tried to hide the pain, but it remained, along with the desire to avenge her mother's murder.

Heartache and longing for home welled within Katherine. She stroked an azure rose from Brittany. Flowers from every planet in the Kingdom of Europa grew in this garden. Her mother had donated crimson roses called the "Lady Charlottes."

Katherine wiped her eyes and strolled on. She hoped to find those roses as she continued her aimless walk along the path.

She knew the politics and intrigue of noble families, and she would play her part. Somehow they would find a way through this trouble. Somehow she would have her revenge against Prince Draven.

As she rounded a curve Katherine caught sight of a man reading an old-fashioned paper book by the light of a glow tree.

"Whoever you are, go away."

Katherine recognized the voice of Prince Magnus.

"Yes, your highness." She turned but didn't hurry away. He had shown interest in her during her last, more pleasant visit, and now he might prove useful. As expected, she heard the scrambling of the prince behind her.

"No, wait. I didn't realize it was you."

A sudden desire for privacy caused Katherine to turn off her bracelet. She looked back over her shoulder. "Me? Yes, it's me. But I can leave if you wish it."

"No. I … uh, I heard you were coming, but no one told me you had arrived."

Still smiling, Katherine turned and curtsied low. He stood a head taller than her, with neatly cut black hair, so unlike the wild hair of his younger brother Prince Draven. "I suppose the formal presentation will be tomorrow, but my family and I arrived a few hours ago."

Prince Magnus nodded. "What brought you to the gardens?"

"Beauty." Katherine stepped closer. "And I couldn't sleep."

"During the summer, I often come here to read."

"I see." Katherine gestured toward the book in his hand. "Is that a paper book?"

Magnus held it out for her. "Yes, one of the oldest in the kingdom, *A history of Mankind from the Diaspora to Unification.*"

She took it and flipped through several pages. "I've read it—not the paper one, but on my palmcomp."

"Really?" Magnus smiled. "Please, sit with me."

Katherine walked with him. "One of my tutors suggested the book. I enjoy reading history."

Magnus positioned two seats next to each other at a small table. "I do also." For a moment he stared at her in silence and then touched her arm. "I'm so very sorry about your mother and, at the same time, I'm glad you don't hate me."

"Why would I hate you?" She placed her hand on his.

"Because of my brother, Draven." Magnus shook his head. "I had no part in what he did or what may come."

Chapter 23

In the palace on Novam Terram

Rachel chafed at the time she lost each day to dressing and undressing, and this morning had already taken longer than usual. "I saw the king yesterday. It was dreadful, and now you're torturing me just because I'm seeing him again."

Anna giggled and pulled on the corset laces. "It's good that you've met the king. Perhaps because of it, our circumstances will change."

"Perhaps for the worse. I'm not who you think I am." Rachel shook her head. "I'm just a scared girl from Earth."

"All you need is faith that the God of Earth can use you."

"Use me? I've been kidnaped, brought to an alien world, tortured, shot …"

Anna pulled again on the corset laces.

"… suffocated in corsets, and the king wants me dead. I don't need any of this. I just want to go home."

"A home and freedom. Isn't that what everyone wants?" Anna tied off the corset.

The king did want Rachel dead, and that terrified her, but he also wanted to eradicate anyone who knew her as Daughter of Earth. She stared at Anna.

"Is there a problem, Lady Rachel?"

"No." Rachel smiled, but sadness lingered behind it. She might eventually cause Anna's death. "You're doing fine."

When fully dressed, Rachel turned before the mirror and admired the layers of lace and the white, silk-like material that flowed from her shoulders to the floor. "This must be the most expensive dress I've ever worn."

Anna nodded and smiled.

Rachel scrunched her face. "But it looks like I'm getting married."

"I can adjust the color."

"You can do that?"

"Yes." Anna felt along the edge of the bodice. "These tabs stitched inside here alter the color."

Moments later, Rachel stood in front of the mirror in the now-emerald green dress. After several turns and glances over her shoulder, she nodded. Still looking in the mirror, Rachel strolled toward a chair, but the shocked look on Anna's face stopped her. "I'm not supposed to sit?"

"No. It might wrinkle the material."

"Spaceships, flying cars, and dresses that change color, but you haven't invented permanent press?" Rachel shook her head. "So, what am I supposed to do until the presentation—just stand here?"

Anna bit her lip. "I'll stand with you, if you like."

"No. You spend too much of the day on your feet for me." Rachel squirmed in the stiff gown. "One of us should be comfortable."

Anna sat but didn't appear relaxed as Rachel ambled around the room. A few minutes later, Sarah appeared and announced that Farold and Lucas were waiting in the hall. Anna jumped to her feet, hurried to the door, and held it wide as Rachel left the room.

Lucas, in his dress uniform, smiled and held out his arm. "You look lovely."

Rachel wrapped her arm on his. "You're the best looking cyborg I've ever seen."

"A what?" Lucas asked.

A stern voice caught Rachel's attention before she could answer, and she glanced over her shoulder.

"Where were you last evening?" Farold stood before his daughter.

Lucas tugged on Rachel's arm, and they walked away, but she could still hear.

"I couldn't sleep so I walked in the gardens."

"With your bracelet turned off?"

Rachel made a mental note to ask Anna how to do that.

"Well, I met Prince Magnus as I walked."

"I need to know where you are and what …."

When they turned the corner, Farold and Katherine's conversation faded.

Farold and a scowling Katherine soon caught up, and the four turned onto a hallway wider than Rachel's living room on Earth. Several hundred lavishly dressed men, women, and a few children lined one side of the corridor talking.

Farold led them to their places near one end.

"So is this a line to get into somewhere?" Rachel asked.

"No." Lucas shook his head. "This is the only time the king comes to us. Some of these people want appointments or favors from King Aelfric. Others, like us, are just letting him know we're here."

"He already knows we're here."

Lucas shrugged. "It's the custom. When the herald says your name, do your best curtsy."

Rachel wanted to say that the king already knew her name, but trumpets sounded, and everyone hurried into a neat line along the wall. Then silence and stillness descended on the chamber like a shroud.

A herald stepped forward. "His Royal Highness King Aelfric, Prince Royal Magnus, and Prince Draven."

The royal trio stepped through the double doors with the herald staying close to king.

Rachel had met the king the day before and Draven more often than she wished, but between them walked a man a couple of years older than her with black, well-trimmed hair. The herald had announced him as Prince Royal Magnus. Rachel liked the look of him—strong, but his face seemed kind, not threatening like ….

Her gaze fell on Prince Draven. She blinked and looked away.

The royal procession continued with those being presented bowing and curtsying like a slow-motion wave in the stands of a football game.

The herald whispered the name of each person as the royals drew near. Sometimes the king smiled, nodded, or occasionally spoke to one of them, but most often he just walked on without any acknowledgement of the person.

"The Marquis of Devon, Lord Admiral Farold Baldwin.

King Aelfric stopped and nodded. "Excellent work saving the Devon system."

"Thank you, Your Highness." Farold replied.

The king stepped to Lucas. "You've become a fine young man. Following in the steps of your brother, are you? You should be seeing Victor soon."

He barely nodded at Katherine as he passed. However, Prince Magnus made up for the lack of attention from his father by leaning close to Katherine and whispering to her.

Katherine's face flushed, and both kept their gazes locked on each other.

The herald came alongside. "Miss Rachel …."

Rachel curtsied.

King Aelfric waved the herald silent and moved on without a glance.

Rachel popped upright. She didn't want to talk to the king, but he didn't have to be rude. She wanted to scream, "Hey, Aelfric, I'm still alive," but instead, she just stood and stared.

No one left after the king passed; they stood and waited in silence. Rachel thought she would die of boredom before the royals disappeared through the doors on the opposite end of the chamber.

Several minutes later, Rachel strolled through the gardens on Lucas's arm. She leaned closer to him. "So are we still confined to the palace?"

"Yes. At least until we come up with a plan to, uh …."

"Kill me?" The words came easily, but fear still boiled within her.

"I'm certain whatever it is will include sparing you. Father tells me he'll be speaking with the king this evening. I think it must have something to do with a plan."

"You *think?*" Rachel stopped. "He hasn't told you?"

Lucas shrugged. "Not yet, anyway."

"Is Katherine part of the plan? Did you notice when Prince Magnus whispered to her how Katherine's face turned red?"

"I did." Lucas shook his head. "It appears she has developed a fondness for him.

"Or Katherine is using him." Rachel smirked. It wouldn't be the first time a woman has toyed with a man to get what she wants."

Lucas frowned.

Rachel leaned close to Lucas again and slowed her pace. "I should go back to my suite. Anna will want to change my clothes before the dinner."

Despite her words, she took smaller steps. She had little desire to return to her suite, a place that felt more like a prison than a palace. The future frightened her.

She smiled at Lucas. This moment was all she wanted.

*   *   *

In a drawing room beside the king's private chambers, Farold poured ale into two tankards.

The king raised his mug. "You know what I like about you, Farold?"

"I would hope to have won your general approval, Your Highness."

The king laughed and then drank deeply. "My advisors always want me to be proper and royal, and I've learned to act that way. But I'm really just an old warrior who likes to drink ale with friends." He shook his head. "I have so few people I can drink with."

Farold wanted to remind the king of those killed in purges or after treason trials. Even more had fled to the borders of the kingdom and beyond. Many of those might have befriended the king if given the chance.

But today, Farold worried for his own family, so he curtailed his response. "I'm glad you're comfortable with me, Your Highness."

After another gulp, the king nodded. "It would be a shame to have to kill you. Do you have a plan for me?"

Farold took his first sip. "I thought I had until tomorrow."

"You do, but we're just two old friends here. If you have an idea, let me know." The king took another deep draft of ale. "Do you remember drinking with me years ago after the Battle of Lyon?"

"I do." Farold took another taste. "It was ten years ago in this very room."

"I said something to you that night that I shouldn't have."

Farold nodded.

"I had you watched for over a year after that. If you had said a word to anyone, you would've been killed. But you never said anything. Do you recall what I told you that night?"

"You said that the Valac had never destroyed the Earth. The Mage kidnapped humans from there, and duped them into fighting for them."

Aelfric cast a sheepish grin. "That's more than I recall saying."

"So we know the Mage lied about Earth, but does anyone know where it is?" Farold took another sip.

"No." Aelfric shook his head. "The Mage hold that as a closely guarded secret. It's the cornerstone of their power. The Mage have told every king that if anyone learns the truth—that Earth remains—and keeps quiet, I should reward them. If they talk, they must die. You kept quiet, and I like you, so I gave you everything I could. But the location of Earth? No human knows that."

Farold smiled and set his tankard down with a clunk. "I know the location of Earth."

Chapter 24

In the palace on Novam Terram

When Rachel awoke the next morning, dread still lingered within her, but she realized things couldn't get much worse, and she couldn't depend on others to improve her situation. She had to find her own solution.

If she discovered a way out of the palace, Farold, Lucas, and Katherine might be able to move on with their lives. She could simply disappear into the huge city and make whatever life she could. She would miss Lucas … and so many others, but Lucas … she would miss him most of all. If her leaving allowed him, and his family, to live it would be worth it.

She pushed back the bed covers.

The plan, what there was of it, had many shortcomings, but she'd heard no better idea since setting foot on this planet.

Anna walked from the closet carrying a mountain of clothes.

Rachel drooped at the sight and pulled off her nightgown. "Sarah, play the most popular music on this planet—loud."

Mellow, classical-like music mixed with a jazzy rhythm filled the room.

"Find something with a quicker beat, and play it louder."

Anna's eyes narrowed, and her pace slowed.

The sound of brass instruments playing a military march filled the room as Rachel held out her bracelet-clad arm and waved Anna closer. "How do you turn this off?"

"Seekers can't deactivate their bracelets, but you can." Anna slid the chemise over Rachel's head and then leaned close to her ear. "Place your thumb on it for several seconds." She pointed to where a watch dial might have been. "After the device senses it's you, a red light will flash. Without taking your thumb off, tap the red light."

Rachel nodded but didn't deactivate it. "Farold used Katherine's to track her. Are the authorities alerted if someone turns it off?"

"No, not for most people." Anna placed the corset around Rachel's waist. "On Devon, Seekers weren't watched, but on this planet they are continuously tracked. Almost no one else is, though." Anna tugged on the laces. "Lord Baldwin must've requested the tracking, but if Lady Katherine had already turned the bracelet off, it wouldn't have shown a location."

"How could she get back into her room without it?"

"Being off only means it doesn't send a signal." Anna knelt, and Rachel stepped into the petticoat. "If Lady Katherine turned her bracelet off, she couldn't open doors remotely, but she could still open them by touching the bracelet to the door."

Anna held the shoes as Rachel slid them on. Then Anna took the hoop skirt from the edge of the bed and Rachel stepped into it.

"Or Lady Katherine might've had a young prince open all the doors for her." Anna's eyes twinkled. "News travels fast in the palace."

She slid a blue dress over Rachel's head and pulled it down.

"Thank you Anna. Pack me clothes and other things for a couple of day and then show me the way to the servant areas of the palace. I'm looking for a way out." Rachel smiled and turned off her bracelet. "You'll be opening all the doors."

Within minutes Rachel descended into cramped and dim rooms, vastly different from the spacious, well-lit palace she knew. A servant rushed along the narrow hall but, seeing Anna, carrying a large bag, and Rachel, he pressed himself against the wall, allowing them room to pass.

"Are all of these people helots?" Rachel used the pejorative term in case she was overheard.

"Most of them." Anna turned a corner. "All of them who live and work down here are Seekers."

It startled Rachel that Anna would use that term so freely in the palace. "Have you told them about me?"

"That you are the Daughter of Earth?" Anna nodded. "Naomi and I both have."

Rachel took as deep a breath as she could in the corset. "I hope you haven't made the situation worse for me by telling them." Rachel stopped. "Have I endangered you by having you show me the way?"

Anna shrugged. "The moment Naomi said you were the Daughter of Earth, I was in danger. Since then our lives have been tied together. If Nightwatch comes for you, they won't leave me behind." She turned and strode on through a dorm area.

Rachel followed, pondering Anna's words and marveling at her bravery.

They continued past more startled servants who scurried out of the way and downstairs to an empty dining area. Seating maybe a hundred, it looked like her high school cafeteria—gray, functional, and antiseptic. A little sunlight shined through barred windows along one wall.

"Do you eat here? Why is it empty?"

"Yes, along with some workmen and the soldiers guarding the palace." Anna wove through the tables. "Everyone has already eaten. That's why it's empty. The cooks are working on lunch."

Rachel shook her head. Lunch already? She hadn't even eaten breakfast yet.

They exited through another door into a gymnasium-size storeroom filled with crates. At the rear, a garage-like door hung above the loading area. Sunlight poured in, promising a way out.

"I'm not supposed to be here, so I don't know what lies beyond, but that's the only exit from the servants' area."

"Thank you. Get back to where you're supposed to be. I hope you'll be fine."

Anna stepped away, but then stopped. "Will I see you again?"

"I don't know." Rachel walked toward the door. Had she abandoned Anna? Would Nightwatch arrest her? Were there cameras recording all of this? "Be careful, Anna."

Anna passed the luggage bag to Rachel, nodded and then hurried away.

Death awaited Rachel in the palace. She had to go.

Rachel pushed herself onward as images of Anna, Naomi, Konrad from the Argonaut, and Lucas, flashed through her mind. She hadn't asked for any of this torment, but she still felt a responsibility. With each step she walked away from people who thought of her as the prophesied Daughter of Earth.

She stopped at the door. "Please, God … is this the right thing to do?" She longed for a sign of some sort, or a voice from—

"Stop!" A soldier ran to the loading dock. "Excuse me, ma'am, but you're not supposed to be here."

Two other soldiers hurried to join him.

"Oh, hello." Rachel didn't like the stereotype, but nevertheless smiled and did her best impression of a dumb blonde. "I was supposed to meet some friends for an outing."

High walls and a solid gate enclosed the warehouse lot. Autowagons moved crates and containers to this dock and several others.

"This is a warehouse and delivery area for the palace and government ministries."

"Can I go find my friends?" Rachel gestured toward the gate.

"You'll need to go back into the palace, ma'am."

Disappointed, she resolved to try another route later and returned to the servants' area. As she reentered the cafeteria, Anna stood by the door.

"I prayed I'd see you again, but I'm surprised it's so soon."

Rachel said nothing as she crossed the room. There seemed to be a universal conspiracy against her.

Smells of foods brought grumbles from her empty stomach. Depression and fear gave way to hunger, and she plopped down at a table near the door to the kitchen. "Can you get me some breakfast?"

"You want to eat here?"

"Why not?" she said flatly and slumped forward, resting her head and arms on the table.

After a minute of silent solitude, loud male voices intruded. She couldn't make out the words and tried to ignore them.

Anna screamed.

Rachel jumped to her feet and ran toward the kitchen. Fear stopped her in the shadowy hallway.

Anna struggled to get away from a man more than twice her age and size. A second, even older man laughed nearby. Three gray-haired, female cooks stood silently along one wall.

Naomi burst into the room through another door. "No! Stop!"

The older man grabbed Naomi by her hair and pulled her to his chest.

Naomi pounded him with her fists to little avail.

Rage overcame fear. Rachel strode into the kitchen and commanded, "Let her go."

"We're just having fun with the helots." The man holding Naomi said, and then twisted her head around and kissed her.

"Yeah. Who are you?" The other man tightened his grip around Anna's breasts and waist.

"The Daughter of Earth!" Rachel looked about, seized a carving knife from the counter, lunged forward, and thrust it deep into his upper arm.

He screamed and released his grip on Anna.

Rachel twisted the knife out, and the man stumbled back. Cursing, he held up a hand in a stop motion.

She plunged the blade through the hand and immediately yanked it out, ready for another thrust.

The man screamed again. Blood flowing from his hand and arm, he stumbled away.

Rachel stepped toward the older man holding Naomi. She snarled, "Release her."

Immediately, he freed Naomi and dashed from the kitchen.

"Are you both okay?" Rachel asked in a calmer voice than what she felt.

Anna and Naomi nodded.

"Who were they?" Rachel dropped the knife, and it clanged on the tile floor.

"Palace laborers," Anna said without emotion.

"Anna happened to be there when they wanted some fun." Naomi's voice dripped with hate. Such things happen all too often to us."

"Are you hurt?" Anna pointed to Rachel's arm.

Blood stained her dress sleeve. "No, I'm fine. However, I won't be eating breakfast this morning." She turned and left.

Trembling and feeling faint, Rachel wandered until she located a hallway she recognized. Then she searched for her suite. Only as she neared the door did she bother to turn the bracelet back on.

Sarah appeared, between her and the door. "Lord Baldwin requires your immediate presence in the emerald drawing room."

Not wanting palace intrigue or even friendly company, Rachel thought about turning the bracelet off again and hiding, but eventually she'd have to face the world. Then she glanced at her blood-splattered sleeve and considered changing. She shook her head. "Lead me there."

A few minutes later, Sarah gestured toward large green doors that opened as Rachel neared. Sarah dissolved as Rachel entered.

Farold, Lucas, and Katherine already sat around a table.

"Why is it that women seem to disappear from the palace?" Farold's disapproving gaze drifted from Rachel to his daughter. Then he motioned for Rachel to join them and tapped the silver null space device in the middle of the table. It hummed and turned green. "King Aelfric asked about our plan last night."

Rachel tried to focus on Farold's words, but the knife encounter still occupied her thoughts.

"We're all to meet with the king this afternoon." Farold gave each a serious stare. "At that time, I'll propose that I transport Rachel and the helots who know about her to Earth and leave them—"

"No one knows the location of Earth." Lucas shook his head.

"I hadn't finished." Farold stared in silence for a moment. "The coordinates were in the crystals you captured at the Aux facility on Lepeus Delta."

Lucas's eyes widened. "I held the location of Earth in my hands and didn't know it?" He turned to Farold. "But you figured it out? We know where Earth is? And we're going there?"

"Not *we*," Farold asserted. "If the king accepts my plan, I alone will escort Rachel to Earth. I want to keep you and Katherine as far from this as possible."

Rachel wanted to be happy about the news of Earth, but she felt only numbness. Still, through a cloud of worry and fear, she needed to speak up.

She held up her bloodstained sleeve. "Before we see the king, you should know that I stabbed a man in the kitchen this morning."

Farold stared at Rachel with narrow angry eyes.

"And I shouted that I was the Daughter of Earth."

Chapter 25

In the palace on Novam Terram

Rachel lowered her bloodstained sleeve. "I didn't kill him ... I'm pretty sure anyway ... I just stabbed him ... twice.

Farold slumped deeper into his seat with each additional revelation. "I may regret asking, but tell me the details." After she finished, he still looked perplexed. "Why were you in that part of the palace?"

"Uh ... sightseeing." It was her first idea, and she immediately knew it wasn't her best.

Farold's eyes narrowed, and his stern face displayed complete disbelief. "We meet with King Aelfric in five hours," he said flatly. "Until then, let's all keep our bracelets on and confine our strolls and sightseeing to the guest wing of the palace."

*　*　*

So many thoughts troubled Lucas's mind that he longed for distraction. He couldn't imagine that on such a warm, sunny day the gardens would be out-of-bounds. Besides, he'd keep his bracelet switched on, so anyone could contact him if they wished.

He wandered among flowers of every imaginable color and then turned down a walkway lined by green hedges. A few yards in, several attractive young ladies in fine-looking gowns strolled across his path. He stopped and bowed. They each curtsied and hurried onward.

Women certainly were a distraction. Most of the women Lucas knew resembled those ladies, attractive and delicate to the point of being fragile.

Rachel was an exception. She wasn't fragile; in some ways, she was strong and even brave. She'd performed courageously in battle aboard the *Argonaut*, days ago on Exeter, and this morning, she had apparently stabbed a man for assaulting Anna.

To avoid a similar outcome, Lucas made a mental note to be kind to Anna.

In spite of her manly qualities of courage and bravery, Rachel possessed beauty from head to toe. He smiled, recalling the first time he'd seen her in the Aux facility on Lepeus Delta—naked. Yes, that had been a sight to behold.

He sighed. Why did his thoughts always return to Rachel when he reflected on beauty and women? He shook his head and tried to think of someone else, but he couldn't.

Rachel reminded him of both his mother and Katherine. Despite the weakness inherent in all females, his mother and Katherine had always remained ready to fight for what they believed in. He admired his sister's steadfast courage.

Rachel probably wouldn't appreciate being compared with other women, but it helped him understand why he liked her so much.

Liked? Lucas frowned. *That was not the right word.*

Still pondering Rachel and his feelings, Lucas stepped near the edge of one of the ponds. Thirty yards away, Rachel ambled toward him along the water's edge.

She stared at something in the pond while he stared at her. He had known women before, but those were mere coquetries. This was something much more profound. He wanted to go to her, hold her, and tell her of his feelings.

But Rachel's life mixed palace intrigue and treason. His father would forbid even a dalliance in Rachel's direction, and if the king accepted his father's plan, they would soon be separated forever.

He sighed and strode away before she spotted him.

*   *   *

Later that day, Rachel would learn how her life would change, but as she walked along the edge of the pond, she struggled to live in the moment. Colorful, glowing, fish-like creatures followed her along the water's edge. She had asked Anna what they were she told her they were glowfish, a simple, but apt name. Even in daylight, the glowfish provided a colorful spectacle.

Some of her experiences since waking up on Lepeus Delta had been horrific, like the tortures inflicted by the Aux, fighting the Valac, and Draven's attempt to kill her, Katherine, and Naomi. But many other things, like the glowfish, were beautiful. But most of all she would miss some of the people, Katherine, Anna, Naomi, Tybalt, Konrad, Farold and Lucas.

Something moved at the edge of her vision. Rachel turned her head.

Lucas disappeared down a pathway between nearby hedges.

For a moment, Rachel wanted to hurry after him, but he must've seen her. *Why did he walk away?*

She knew this culture was more conservative than back home in Seattle, but he *did* like her, and perhaps felt more. She hoped he did.

But what was the point of opening her heart to him? If King Aelfric agreed, Farold would soon take her back to Earth and leave her there. If the king didn't agree, she would be taken out and shot, or whatever they did on this world. She hesitated to think of the possible forms of execution.

Perhaps it was better this way. Why should she ask Lucas to open his heart only to have it hurt, and why should she expose her own?

Yet despite those fears, she longed to express the feelings that grew daily within her. And, even if for just a day, she wanted to know for certain how Lucas felt about her.

*　*　*

At the appointed time, they returned to the chamber where Rachel had first met King Aelfric. Farold and Lucas entered first, followed by Katherine and Rachel.

Prince Draven waited inside along with another man who stood tall and had a short, dark beard.

"Victor!" Farold smiled and held out his hand.

Victor shook his hand but didn't smile. "Hello, Father."

The king entered before their discussion could progress beyond the greeting. Everyone bowed or curtsied, and all attention turned to him.

"Be seated everyone. I have two requirements."

Farold remained standing as all others sat.

The king sat in his grand chair on the platform. "First, the Earth girl must be removed and, second, the helots who have come to believe in her nonsense must be dealt with. Lord Baldwin, what do you propose?"

"Your Highness, as you required, I have come up with a plan," Farold began. "Using information from the crystals recovered on Lepeus Delta, I have ascertained a location for Earth on the far side of the Great Nebula.

"If Your Highness approves, I'll take the Veritas and transport Rachel and the few helots who harbor treasonous delusions about her, to Earth and leave them there. That will alleviate the problem of the both Rachel and the helots who have fallen under her sway. In so doing, I will also confirm the existence of Earth and bring back that information to you."

King Aelfric nodded. "What assurance do I have that you will do exactly that?"

Spreading his arms wide, Farold spoke as if the king had impugned his honor. "Your Highness, I have always been your loyal servant, but if you need additional assurance, my sons and daughter will remain here, in the kingdom of Europa. I wouldn't leave my children here to pay the price of my disloyalty."

Again the king nodded. "What if there is no Earth?"

"Rachel and the helots will never return to any of the Kingdoms of Terra."

The king rested his chin in one hand and stared off to the side for several moments. Then, in a flat, even, tone, he said, "No."

Chapter 26

In the palace on Novam Terram

Silence gripped the room.

Farold's eyes widened and he shook his head. "Forgive me for asking Your Highness, but how does my plan fail you?"

"The journey will be long and dangerous. If you disappeared for several months or perhaps never returned, there would be talk. However, sons go off to battle and many never return. If Victor and Lucas died during the mission, a plausible story could be spread about their deaths. They will go in your place."

Farold stepped closer. "Your Highness, I assure you—"

"That is my decision." The king waved him to a stop. He focused his gaze on Victor and Lucas. "You will remove the irritation of this girl and the traitors and return with proof that Earth exists. If you fail, your Father and sister will die, and your lands and titles will be forfeited. Do you understand?"

"Yes, Your Highness," Victor replied.

With a nod, Lucas mumbled the same.

"Also, I heard of a knife attack against a palace worker this morning." King Aelfric stared at Rachel. "It seems this as-yet unidentified female assailant called herself the Daughter of Earth. All the servants are whispering about it. It appears we will need to provide another vessel for the additional helots we will be transporting."

In a softer, almost fatherly voice, the king spoke to Katherine. "Before all this treason and nastiness, my son Draven spoke fondly of you. Perhaps a marriage uniting our two houses might be beneficial."

Katherine glanced at Prince Draven and managed a weak smile.

Rachel felt nauseated at the thought.

"However, such pleasantries will have to wait," the king continued. "Draven, you will accompany the expedition as my personal envoy. Ensure the Earth girl and helots are gone forever and that the location and evidence of Earth are provided to me."

Draven mouth gaped at his Father's order to accompany the mission, but he regained his composure and said, "Whatever you wish, Father."

King Aelfric turned to Victor. "Earlier, I promised you a promotion to major. I've changed my mind. I'm promoting you to colonel and placing you in charge of all marines on the expedition, including your brother Lucas."

"Thank you, Your Highness." Victor smiled.

The king returned his attention to Farold. "I'll be presenting honors to both you at Victor at the Ceremony of Heroes in two days. Also, since your daughter and you will remain as guests here, we will use the *Veritas* on this expedition. Have your sons and the Earth girl ready to depart in …." He turned to Draven. "Is three days enough time?"

"Yes, Father." Draven bowed. "I'll be ready to leave with the traitors at that time."

After the meeting, Farold waited in the Privy Council chamber, anxious to speak with Victor.

However, the moment the king departed, Prince Draven hurried to Victor and engaged him in conversation about the expedition to Earth.

From nearby, Farold watched the confusion and consternation on Victor's face. It seemed clear to Farold that Victor knew little about Earth's existence or the mission he had been assigned.

"Go now and assemble the supplies your marines will need," Draven said to Victor. "I'll meet with you this afternoon to discuss additional plans."

Victor bowed and left without a glance at his father.

Farold turned to follow.

"Wait, please, Lord Baldwin."

Gritting his teeth, Farold stopped and faced Prince Draven.

"Your son has not engaged in any of your treason, and I want to keep it that way." Draven stepped closer. "He and I will be spending most of the next few days together in preparation for this mission. Any time spent with you would be suspect and could endanger him. Keep that in mind."

Farold left the room convinced he'd been thoroughly outmaneuvered.

*   *   *

Two days later, Rachel strolled out of the palace on Lucas's arm. Ahead of them, Katherine walked with Prince Magnus.

"Remember the line of lights when we landed?" Lucas smiled and squeezed her hand. "I think you called it a runway. Well, it's called the Avenue of Heroes, and it runs along one side of the palace. It's there, during the Ceremony of Heroes, that the king presents military awards."

Rachel looked over her shoulder at the five palace guards and smirked. "So nice of King Aelfric to ensure our safety during this long walk."

Lucas leaned close. "Think of them as protection for Prince Magnus."

Rachel mouthed, "Sure," and then grinned. "It will be nice to see your father receive an award."

Lucas nodded.

They departed the palace on a skywalk that loomed over a surface road. The skywalk led to the top of the nearby mammoth structure.

The Avenue of Heroes had a wide paved area with seating rising up on either side, like a coliseum. Perhaps it was an elongated stadium or like the Circus Maximus she'd read about in world history class.

Drummers and trumpeters lined both sides of the broad lane.

Still with Lucas, Rachel the others strolled down a covered walkway along one side of the avenue. Below, thousands of people filled the seats.

"A great day for football."

"Football?" Lucas asked.

"Just a game." Rachel smiled. "But I hope someday I can show you. I think you'd like it."

Magnus stepped next to the door, and a device scanned his eye. The door slid open, revealing a waiting lift. Everyone filed in and it dropped, quicker than Rachel's stomach would've liked. When it stopped, Prince Magnus led them to a private seating area about midway up the stands.

The four entered, leaving the guards outside.

Their booth during the Last Night ceremony on Exeter had been nice, but the deep carpets, plush seats, and carved wooden tables here exceeded its luxury. Rachel sat next to Lucas with Katherine on her right. Prince Magnus sat on the other side of Katherine.

From this location, high above, but near one end of the elongated stadium, Rachel had a perfect view of the entire scene. Just to her right, at one end of the venue, a grand, two-story portico rose above the stone avenue.

Two thrones sat near the railing with additional, less ornate seating extending in an arc behind them. On each side stood a huge statue of an angel; complete with robes and white feathery wings. Each angel held a flag in one hand and a sword in the other. Rachel guessed the statues towered fifty feet high.

Below and in front of the portico, as if in an orchestra pit, technicians worked with computares.

"That's the royal seating area." Lucas gestured toward the thrones. "King Aelfric and Queen Miriam will view the ceremony from there."

Magnus leaned forward. "My mother left for Turriff before you arrived."

"I'm surprised your father let us attend." Rachel felt her face flush, but Magnus didn't seem offended.

"He didn't want any of you out of the palace, but I thought you'd want to see this." Prince Magnus frowned. "Father insisted on the guards."

Rachel cast Lucas an "I told you so," glare.

Katherine smiled. "I'm glad you could arrange this for us."

From the moment Rachel met her, Katherine had been infatuated with Tybalt. They were all still in peril, and Katherine would have to remain in the palace. Could her current flirtations with Prince Magnus be just an act to gain favor?

Rachel pointed to the statues. "What do they symbolize?"

"Oh, they're much more than symbols," Lucas replied.

King Aelfric stepped to the edge of the portico, and the trumpets blared before Lucas could continue. The baritone beat of the drums followed, and the crowd jumped to their feet with a thunderous roar. The others in the booth stood, and Rachel followed suit.

As the cheers faded, King Aelfric gave a slight nod to the technicians below him and then returned his gaze to the crowd. His voice boomed. "Let the recognition of heroes begin."

One man marched to the center of the pavement below and sang the anthem Rachel had heard at the Last

Night ceremony. When he finished, the stone wall that hid the technicians ignited in a giant vid display of King Aelfric as he smiled and waved.

Rachel turned her gaze to the other end of the coliseum where large double doors slid open, and twenty men, all in military uniform, marched out to the beat of the drummers. They strode along the pavement between the trumpeters, the drummers, and the roaring crowd. As the soldiers drew closer, Rachel spotted Farold standing next to Victor near the front of the column.

When the marchers were right below their booth, Rachel could see the entire royal portico and all the men marching without the slightest turn of her head.

Light burst from the two angel statues, and they transformed into giant lifelike angels. The images were so real Rachel believed it to be some sort of holo projection.

Both angels gazed down with approval at the approaching men.

Rachel gasped. "Wow … did the technicians do that? This is way better than Hollywood." Rachel leaned forward. "I only see the giant moving angels, not the statues. How did they do that?"

"I wish I knew how it happens." Lucas's eyes narrowed at the giant figures. "It's not controlled by anyone here. The Mage sometimes do this during ceremonies."

"It's the most public way that the Mage communicate with us," Magnus added.

"The Mage look like angels?" Rachel asked.

"Usually shorter ones." Lucas shrugged. "No one actually knows what they look like. We believe this is some form of holo-imaging. We don't know how they're doing it, but they always appear like this—as angels."

"You're fighting a war for an alien race you've never actually seen?"

"History says that the Mage saved us from the Valac." Magnus shrugged. "Most people never doubt what they're taught. So, for them, what does it matter what the Mage look like? Perhaps they are angels."

Rachel thought demons were the more likely answer. Surely his father had told him the truth, that the Valac hadn't destroyed Earth and that the Mage were liars.

She turned toward Magnus, ready to confront him, but she held back. Tomorrow she would leave this star kingdom forever. What point would an interrogation of the prince royal serve? She leaned back in her seat.

Moments later, stairs extended from both sides of the royal platform. One at a time, the twenty men marched up the stairs, were announced, and received medals, promotions, or titles.

"Lord Admiral Farold Baldwin," the herald announced. "For conspicuous bravery in the defense of the Devon system and victory over a superior Valac fleet, King Aelfric hereby awards you the Ruby Cross of the Guardian Knights of Terra."

As Farold exited on the one side, with the medal pinned to his uniform, Victor climbed the stairs on the other.

"Viscount Lord Lieutenant Victor Baldwin," the herald continued. "For conspicuous bravery in the defense of the Draconis system, King Aelfric hereby promotes you to colonel and awards you the Bronze Cross of the Guardian Knights of Terra."

After the last man received his award, the closest Mage angel stepped forward and spoke to the crowd. "While we are proud of these fine warriors who fight to protect us all from the savagery of the Valac hegemony, there is evil within the Kingdom of Europa."

The crowd gasped.

The second Mage angel then stepped forward. "Even now, the helots are spreading their lies. Even now, some of the great among you are succumbing to the allure of evil. A swift death must be their only reward."

Shouts of agreement thundered through the audience.

The gazes of both angels swept along the crowd, but had their accusing stares lingered on her?

Rachel's averted her gaze and slouched deep into her seat.

* * *

"That was a nice ceremony." Katherine smiled at Magnus as she walked across the drawing room with two glasses of wine. Cultivating a good relationship with the future king had seemed like a good idea. Such a plan appeared especially prudent now that she'd be staying in the palace for several months.

However, what had started as a strategy to help her and possibly save the whole family had become something greater. The more time she spent with Prince Magnus, the more she enjoyed his company.

She handed him a glass and sat close beside him, imagining her father's disapproval.

Magnus took a sip and set the glass down. "I often come here to read and watch the sunset."

She smiled and set her glass aside. Now that they were alone she needed answers. While she knew many of his opinions and ideas, the current controversy regarding Earth and Rachel had remained untouched. Katherine wanted to know his thoughts, but she feared placing herself in greater danger, or at least damaging this new friendship.

Tentatively, she broached the subject. "You know that Rachel says she's from Earth."

Magnus nodded.

"An Earth much more advanced than the one our ancestors left."

"Yes." His eyes narrowed. "I've kept informed about her."

"So do you believe that Earth—?"

The door opened with a swish.

Katherine turned toward it.

Two Nightwatch soldiers burst in and fired lances.

As darkness swept over her, Katherine collapsed to the floor.

Chapter 27

On Novam Terram

Prince Draven sat rolling a pen back and forth along on his father's desk. The Mage were eager for the transfer of power and required him to act quickly. His plan would unfold over the next few hours, but he had not devised it in haste. He had dwelled on portions of the plot for many years.

In the morning he would announce the murder of his father King Aelfric. All the evidence would point to a conspiracy between his older brother Magnus and Lord Farold Baldwin. Magnus's bracelet would show that he had boarded a dart with Katherine and other members of the Baldwin family.

After the announcement of the king's murder, and the revelation of the evidence against Magnus and Baldwin family, Draven would have Farold arrested and quickly executed. The traitor's ships would be destroyed in battle. To most of the citizens of Europa, it would appear to have been a failed coup led by Magnus.

Draven leaned back in the large comfortable chair. Soon those who stood in his way would be dead, leaving him king of Europa. He looked down at his father's body on the floor and smiled.

*   *   *

In the predawn twilight, Rachel walked across the dartpad. Men and autowagons moved supplies onto the Baldwin family dart and onto another military dart nearby.

Prince Draven exited the Baldwin craft.

Rachel ducked behind a vehicle and watched as Prince Draven rushed over to Victor, about a hundred yards away. The two men talked briefly, then Draven hurried toward nearby buildings.

Someone touched Rachel's arm, and she spun around with her fists clenched.

Lucas stumbled back. "It's just me. Put the knife away."

"You're lucky I don't have one." Rachel glanced back, looking for Draven, but he had disappeared. With the prince gone, she relaxed a bit and turned to Lucas. "I'm sorry. I'm still nervous … afraid, really. Until we leave, try not to surprise me." She looked him up and down. "Why are you in uniform?"

"This is a military expedition. I'm going to be on duty. Why were you hiding here? Were you spying on someone?"

"Prince Draven. I spotted him coming out of your dart, and then he talked to Victor, but I don't see him now." She pointed to Victor. "Have you talked with your brother?"

"No." Lucas took her arm and together they continued toward the dart. "I've tried to, but he just says, 'Not now,' and walks away."

"I'm sorry."

"It's not your fault."

"It sort of is. If I hadn't—"

"If you hadn't been kidnapped by the Aux … if you hadn't lived through all they did to you … If I hadn't found you. Let's not go over it all again. It's not your fault."

Prince Draven exited a nearby storeroom into the growing daylight. An autowagon carrying two oblong crates, emblazoned with golden royal seals, followed him.

Lucas sneered. "Those cases probably contain his clothes for the journey."

Rachel laughed. "When are we flying to the *Veritas*?"

"Soon." Lucas looked around. "I'd hoped that Father and Katherine would be here to see us off."

"You haven't seen them this morning?"

Lucas shook his head as stopped at the foot of the ramp. He turned and faced Rachel. "They weren't in their rooms. I thought they'd be here."

"Does that worry you?" It concerned Rachel.

"A bit, but we've probably just missed each other."

Rachel frowned. "Anna didn't show up this morning."

His face tighened at her words, but he smiled. "I'm sure she's fine."

Rachel had said goodbye and hugged Katherine at dinner the night before, but she'd waited to say farewell to Anna and Naomi. Farold hadn't even been at dinner.

Now she wanted to see and hug them all—even Farold, who would probably be very stiff and formal about it.

"I wonder if King Aelfric is trying to keep us apart." She gestured toward Draven. "Will he be with us on the *Veritas*?"

"No." Lucas stopped at the foot of the dart ramp and spoke softly. "The *Argonaut* arrived, and he'll be on that vessel with Victor. Evidently, they arrested and loaded over a thousand Seekers into the hold of the ship before it left Exeter."

Rachel's eyes flared wide.

"And they loaded more this morning. Anna and Naomi might already be onboard. Also, two other ships will escort—"

Rachel held up her hand. "Why didn't you tell me about the Seekers before now?" Her stomach churned with anxiety and guilt.

"You knew King Aelfric would have Draven round up those who knew about you."

"I guess I didn't think it would be so many."

"I asked Victor, and even Prince Draven, about the conditions on the ship. They both said they didn't know. I'm hoping they've planned and provisioned the trip well."

"Really?" Rachel shook her head. "A thousand Seeker men, women and children in the hold of the *Argonaut*— that's bad."

Webber, the usual family pilot, stepped out from the dart. "We're ready to leave when you are, sir."

Lucas looked from one side of the dartpad to the other. "Come on. Let's get on board."

Rachel followed him up the ramp, but it didn't feel right to leave without saying a last goodbye. She might see Anna and Naomi in the days ahead, but she would never see Farold or Katherine again. Had something bad happened to them, or was this all part of King Aelfric's plan? Or both? Had he thrown them in the dungeon? "Is there a dungeon in the palace?"

"What?" Lucas shook his head. "No."

As Rachel stepped through the hatch, Anna and Naomi came into the view, cuffed to their seats. Rachel stormed through to the pilots. "Which of you has the key?" she demanded.

Webber looked to the younger man beside him.

"Uh, Prince Draven ordered it," the young man said. "He wanted to ensure they stayed in the dart."

Rachel held out her hand. "Hand it over."

The young man passed her the key.

After releasing her friends, Rachel asked them if Draven had left any packages behind.

With puzzled looks, they both shook their heads.

Despite their assurances and feeling a bit paranoid, Rachel checked for bombs. She found none, and the dart lifted off. She spent most of the flight imagining how and where she might chain Draven.

As she calmed, her thoughts turned to all the Seekers on the *Argonaut*. Were they chained up like slaves in the hold of the ship?

She shook her head and turned to Lucas. "Are the Seekers on the *Argonaut* chained?"

"I don't know."

"I have to know." She stared at the deck. "I have to know how bad it is."

Lucas nodded and ordered the course change.

Several minutes later the dart clanged to rest in the *Argonaut* docking bay. The four stepped to the rear of the craft as the ramp slid down,

Victor stood outside waiting. "What are you doing here?" he growled. "My orders were that you remain on the *Veritas*."

Lucas stepped closer. "We need to talk."

"Yes, we certainly do, and now seems a good time." Victor strode up the ramp. "Back inside the dart. We'll talk, and then you and these others will leave." Victor ordered the pilots out and then turned to Rachel. "You and the helots—"

"We're staying." Rachel crossed her arms. "We know everything you're likely to discuss."

Victor grunted.

Lucas raised the ramp.

The moment they were alone in the dart, Victor bellowed, "How did you get involved in this insanity, this treason?"

Lucas stepped back. "I don't know what Draven has told you, but it's a lie."

"Why would he lie about Father and you?"

"I don't know, but he did." He turned to Rachel. "Do you still have the crystal with you?"

Rachel nodded.

"I think it's best that Victor sees the evidence."

"Must *everyone* in the Kingdom of Europa see me naked?" She retrieved the crystal from her bodice and handed it to Lucas.

Lucas inserted it in a computare and leaned close to the scanner. "I just hope we can open this."

It scanned Rachel's hand and eye, then light shimmered, and a motionless holo projection of Tybalt appeared in the middle of the dart.

Victor groaned "Tybalt is involved in this conspiracy, too?"

Rachel strode toward the pilot compartment. "We think of it as searching for truth, but yes, he is. Oh, and in a minute or two, try not to ogle me too much, okay?"

"What?" Victor's eyes narrowed. "You are indeed a crazy woman."

Wanting company and knowing that her naked holo image would soon appear on the display, Rachel called for Anna and Naomi to join her and then shut the door.

*   *   *

Alone with his brother in the rear compartment of the dart, Lucas rolled the crystal in his hand. "I want you to watch this."

"What possible justification can you have for helping this lunatic live out her fantasies of Earth?" Victor asked.

Lucas tapped the computare controls. "Please, just watch this."

The holo projection of Tybalt moved and spoke. "Dearest Katherine I have a significant favor to ask of you. The lady that hopefully now stands beside you needs to be protected. Lucas found her after a battle for an Aux base on planet Lepeus Delta …."

"Tybalt, my friend and former squire—a traitor." Victor grunted.

When the image stopped, Lucas tapped the display once again. "There's more. Please keep an open mind."

After Tybalt, the projection dissolved and reformed into a rotating blue and green planet.

Lucas stepped closer and pointed. "Rachel says this is Earth."

Victor walked in a circle around the projection. "Some of it is similar to the ancient maps." He shook his head. "But most is completely unfamiliar."

After several rotations of the planet, the picture faded, and a holoprojection of a naked Rachel replaced it. Her arms and legs lay spread wide and motionless, but her eyes danced with fear. The likeness turned slowly, revealing every inch of her.

"Rachel knew I would be seeing this?"

"Yes."

"You found this, and her, on Lepeus Delta?"

Lucas nodded.

"Is she restrained in some way?"

"She doesn't remember much from this time, and nothing of this. I think the Aux had control of parts of her brain."

"Really?"

"It's just a guess, but it would explain what we're seeing."

Gradually, Victor shifted his gaze to Lucas. "When we were marching together along the Avenue of Heroes, Father said you had proof of Earth. I didn't believe … didn't want to believe him."

For a few seconds, Aux text scrolled, followed by more images of a naked Rachel, bound to a crystal slab. Four Aux examined her. Next, Rachel appeared as before, with her arms and legs spread wide, but this time the Earth and a moon rotated in unison with her.

Victor pointed to the Aux writing beside each, "Human 7562, Earth, and Luna."

"I didn't know you could read Aux."

Victor turned to Lucas. "It seems we both have much to learn about each other."

Lucas pointed to the display. "The next part shows her abduction."

Text scrolled beside the Earth. The view centered over an area of the planet Rachel had described as her home. Then it zipped down toward the planet surface and stopped a few feet above Rachel. She hurried along in an attractive blue dress that revealed her shoulders, then she looked up with frightened eyes. The image dissolved.

"Do you believe now?"

"I believe King Aelfric believes. Late yesterday he he gave me the coordinates for Earth." Victor tapped the computare and then pointed to part of the Aux text. "These are those coordinates."

It was a start. Lucas smiled with relief.

Victor remained silent for a moment but then tapped his palmcomp. "Signal the *Veritas* that Cornet Lucas, Rachel, and two helots are safe aboard the *Argonaut*."

"Aye, sir," the voice at the other end replied. "Also, sir, the *Vigilant* has suffered an engine malfunction, and so our first jump has been delayed."

For several minutes the brothers continued to discuss the expedition and the possibility of Earth existing.

A motor whined, and the ramp inched downward.

Surprised, Lucas closed the holo image, turned off his palmcomp and slipped the crystal into a pocket.

Before the ramp completely dropped, marines jumped onto it and rushed in with lances at the ready.

A lieutenant stepped forward with his hand lance pointed at Victor. "Sir, Captain Marin has ordered both of you arrested."

Chapter 28

In the Novam Terram star system

Rachel hadn't wanted to see the awful images recorded on the crystal, so she waited in the pilot area with Anna and Naomi. She tried to ignore the arguing in the next compartment and sighed with relief when the volume dropped to an inaudible level.

After several more minutes, she heard the whine of the ramp as it dropped. She thought Lucas would invite them back, but when he didn't, Rachel cracked open the hatch and peeked through. Only dim emergency lights illuminated the rear compartment, but they provided enough illumination to show an empty chamber and landing bay.

Rachel placed her hands on her hips and shook her head. Victor might want to ignore her, but she hardly expected Lucas to have forgotten her.

She wasn't supposed to be on this ship, but her personal mission remained. Rachel faced Anna and Naomi. "Let's find the Seekers."

Naomi jumped to her feet and followed.

Anna rose, more hesitant. "Do you know your way?"

"A little bit. I spent a few days in the brig here." Rachel grinned. "I also know where the Seekers who work onboard live."

To move around the ship without raising questions, Rachel knew she must appear as a lady of high rank on a mission. She took a deep breath and assumed her most haughty poise. "Stay behind me, and don't make eye contact with anyone."

Together they strode with a purposeful air along a main passageway, past several surprised sailors, and then down three levels to a gray, dimly lit corridor.

A bead of sweat rolled along Rachel's cheek. It would be hard for any crewmember to believe that a lady of rank had a mission in this hot and humid section of the ship, but fortunately none of the crew ventured here.

Rachel pointed to the hatch in the deck. "Their quarters are down there. I'll go first; they know me."

Her heels wobbled on the ladder rungs, and her dress crawled up as she descended; she had to brush it down several times. The previous time she'd been here, she'd worn men's clothes, and she'd jumped down the last couple of feet. She wouldn't do that today.

Only dim light illuminated the compartment, just as it had been months ago when she first descended the ladder. Naomi and Anna struggled down the ladder while Rachel stood, allowing her eyes to adjust. As more became visible to her, Rachel noticed a man standing in the corner with a large wrench in his hand.

I need to start carrying a knife. Rachel struggled to maintain her lady of influence poise. "I'm the Daughter of Earth. Who are you?"

"Name's Fray." He slapped the wrench in his palm a couple of times. "Daughter of Earth? He stood silent in the shadows for a moment. "You been on this ship before?"

"Yes, I have. Take me to Konrad."

Fray nodded. "So either old Konrad isn't crazy, or you both are." He waved the wrench. "This way. Some of the crew beat Konrad up a bit."

Rachel hurried past Fray into the next compartment and found a small group of Seekers standing inside. She recognized several faces and then spotted Konrad sitting in the corner wiping his face with a rag.

His eyes widened as they stared at each other.

"Are you okay?" Rachel hurried to his side.

"It's just a few bruises and some teeth knocked out." The words whistled through the gaps. "They'll grow back."

"Yes Konrad. They will." She grinned and leaned closer.

"Where have you been, Daughter of Earth?" Konrad tossed the rag into a nearby bucket. "What have you been doing, and most important of all, why are you back aboard the *Argonaut*?"

After giving him a recap of the last couple of months, she said, "I'm here to see the Seekers in the hold. Can one of your people take me there?"

Konrad stood. "I will. Fray, come with us." He waved to Rachel, Naomi, and Anna. "Follow me."

Fray rested the wrench on his shoulder like a soldier with a lance and followed behind them.

"Nightwatch arrested hundreds on Exeter and loaded them on the ship." Konrad shook his head. "We've been bringing them food and water, but it isn't enough. Some have already died."

They descended another ladder to a narrow walkway that ran between two parts of the *Argonaut's* multi-story engine. It pulsated with energy as the shaft below them spun faster and faster. Rachel's hair frizzed, and her skin tingled.

When they all reached the far side of the engine, Konrad stopped and faced Rachel. "Can you get us past the guards at the entrance to the hold?"

"I'm not sure."

"Then from here we must crawl." Konrad bent over, pulled a grate from the deck, and slipped into what looked like an air vent. Rachel followed and again lamented her long dress as she struggled to crawl. They crept less than twenty feet, but by the end, the stench of urine and feces assaulted Rachel's nostrils.

They stopped their crawl where a large steel grate lay inches from their heads. At Konrad's request several men lifted it from the deck, and then Konrad stood and helped lift Rachel from the vent.

Rachel stood on a box to get a better view. Hundreds of men, women, and children, many wearing only rags, stood within sight of her. They weren't chained, but that amounted to little comfort. They were packed in so tight that only a few could've sat or slept at a time. The heat from the multitude of people mixing with the foul air created a noxious combination.

Konrad lifted Naomi from the vent, and she asked, "If it's so easy to get in here, why don't they escape?"

"We removed the bolts from the grate to make passing food and water easier, but if those imprisoned in the hold did get out where would they go?" Konrad said. "Even if a hundred left through the vent, they'd be hunted down and returned, if not killed."

Sweat rolled down Rachel's face, and her nose and lungs burned. *God, what can I do? How can I help?* She stepped off the box with a growing sense of rage, now mixed with hopelessness, she pushed into the crowd, determined to see the entire hold.

"Wait for us," Naomi called.

"Follow her," Konrad said.

Tears welled in Rachel's eyes, both from anger and the ammonia-laced air as she wove through the crowd.

"Konrad, who is that lady?" a woman called.

A child tugged on Rachel's dress. "Who are you?"

"My name is Rachel." She ran her fingers through the child's matted hair.

"Naomi?" A familiar voice called out.

Joshua, Naomi's father, squeezed past Rachel and embraced his daughter. He slid a hand through his disheveled hair. One sleeve of his shirt hung torn and loose. "I feared I'd never see you again." He hugged her again and then looked to Rachel. "Thank you for bringing her to me, Daughter of Earth."

Many in the crowd gasped at the words, but several cursed.

One shouted, "Why did you do this to us?"

As other family and friends joined in tearful reunion, Joshua beckoned Rachel, Naomi, and Anna. "Come. I must show you something."

Joshua pushed through the throng of people and stopped by an oblong crate with the royal seal printed in gold on the side.

Rachel stopped a few yards away. *Why is Draven's crate here?*

Joshua knelt beside the crate. "Rachel is here. Stay calm, and we'll find a way to get you out." He turned to Rachel. "Lady Katherine is inside."

"*What?* How?" Rachel ran to the large coffin-like box and knelt. "Katherine, are you okay? Get her out!"

"It's locked." Joshua fingered the metal device. "We have no tools."

"Fray, I need you and that wrench," Rachel called over her shoulder.

He hurried to the crate. "I'm happy to break anything with a royal seal on it. Stand back."

Two swings later, Joshua lifted the lid.

Katherine lay sprawled inside with her clothes drenched in sweat. Rachel bent into the box and, with the help of Joshua and Fray, lifted her from inside.

A woman brought over a half-cup of warm water.

"What happened? Have you been drugged? Did Draven put you in there?" Rachel cradled Katherine in her arms and put the cup to her lips. "Drink the water. Please wake up."

"There's another crate over here." Joshua pointed. "But we've heard nothing from inside."

Fray smiled, rushed over, and slammed his wrench against the lock. "There's someone in here too."

Naomi looked inside and gasped. "This is Prince Magnus, but I'm not sure he's alive."

Rachel tapped on her bracelet. "I've got to tell Lucas."

* * *

Lucas could imagine many reasons why he might be arrested, but none involved Victor. Also, he expected to be taken to the brig, but the marines that surrounded them weren't going that way. "Where are we being taken?"

Victor gave him a questioning glance.

"I served on this ship," Lucas whispered. "This isn't the way to the brig."

Victor reduced his pace. "Lieutenant Hale, we're on an expedition by order of King Aelfric. Why have we been arrested? What is the charge against us?"

A marine pushed Victor, but he continued his unhurried pace, and the others slowed to match it.

Lieutenant Hale stopped and faced Victor. "King Aelfric is dead at the hand of your father, Lord Baldwin. Draven is king now and all of your family will be arrested and tried for treason."

"I'm no traitor!" Lucas pushed the nearest marine away. "And if King Aelfric is dead then Prince Magnus should be king."

"Prince Magnus paid your father to kill King Aelfric." The marine shoved Lucas. "Move, traitor."

Lucas stumbled forward, shaking his head. What had he just heard? Could it be true? King Aelfric dead? As much as Lucas disliked the king, a coup in the Kingdom of Europa seemed unimaginable. He shook his head. It couldn't be true. No amount of money could induce his father to kill King Aelfric. They had an agreement, a plan.

As they continued down the passageway Lucas tried not to imagine what might now happen to his father and Katherine.

As the group continued through the ship, Lucas realized the marines were taking them to the captain's stateroom. When they arrived, the lieutenant and three marine guards ushered Lucas and Victor inside.

Captain Marin sat reading his palmcomp for nearly a minute, then he looked up. "As you have certainly heard, King Aelfric is dead. Victor, you were aboard this ship when the king was murdered this morning, and I will testify to that fact, but Lucas …." He shook his head. "It's sad to see a great family brought down by such folly."

"My brother had nothing to do with the death of King Aelfric or any other treason," Victor declared.

"Your loyalty to your brother is commendable, but ill-advised." With a cold, stony look Captain Marin continued, "Your father was the last one seen with the king. I've been ordered to hold you both on charges of treason and to transport you back to Novam Terram. You'll be taken to the brig until—"

The ethercomm on the sleeve of Lucas's uniform vibrated. Without looking, Lucas reached over to disconnect the call but must've tapped the wrong spot.

A female voice said, "Lucas, I'm in the hold, and Katherine is here …"

"Shut that thing off," the captain ordered.

"… and Prince Magnus. I think they were shot. Katherine is barely awake. Magnus is unconscious."

Lucas held his finger over the control but stopped. "Prince Magnus is in the hold with you?"

"Yes, on the *Argonaut*. He's in a crate that I saw Draven load on a dart this morning."

Captain Marin pointed to the ethercomm. "Who is that woman?"

"Uh …" Lucas decided against identifying Rachel as the crazy woman they had found on Lepeus Delta. "A friend."

Victor coughed. "Excuse me, sir, but if Prince Magnus is locked in our hold it would seem he had nothing to do with the death of King Aelfric. Magnus is our king, not Prince Draven."

Captain Marin nodded. "I need to see this unconscious person. All of you come with me. Lieutenant Hale, summon security to the hold—now!"

"Yes, sir." As he followed the captain along the passageway, Hale spoke into his ethercomm.

The alert signal sounded over the vox. "Security Alert! Security Alert! Away the master-at-arms force to the hold. All marines report to the hold."

Lucas had never before seen Captain Marin run—actually run—but he did then. Victor hurried to keep pace, and Lucas followed a few yards back. No one guarded either of them as the throng descended several levels and continued aft.

More marines joined the flow as they ran, and Tybalt came alongside Lucas.

"I heard about King Aelfric. I'm glad to see you're okay," he said. "Why are we running to the hold?"

Lucas explained.

"Rachel is in there with Katherine and Prince Magnus?"

"Yes." Lucas nodded as the hatch came into view.

"Open it," Captain Marin ordered.

The hatch swung away, and foul air slapped Lucas in the face. Rachel and Katherine were somehow down in that humid abyss? Lucas pushed forward as the master-at-arms force entered. Captain Marin rubbed his nose as he stepped in. Victor, Hale, and Tybalt went next, and then Lucas entered, struggling not to gag. Other marines followed and pushed the Seekers back at lance point.

"Rachel?" Lucas shouted and elbowed his way into the crowd. "Rachel?"

"Lucas!"

"Rachel?" He heard her but, through the mass of humanity, Lucas couldn't see her.

Several pointed him in the right direction.

He continued shoving his way through the people until he spotted her sitting on the deck holding Katherine. Nearby, a well-dressed man lay on the deck with others kneeling around him.

Lucas ran to Rachel. "Will she be okay?" He leaned in close. "What happened?"

Katherine's eyes fluttered, and she gasped. "Stunned … I think. Maybe drugged."

Tybalt joined Lucas. "Let's get her to sickbay."

Captain Marin stepped over to the man on the deck. "By the God of Earth, that is Prince Magnus! Get him out of here. Where's the medicus?" He tapped his ethercomm. "Get the doctor to the hold—now!"

"Yes, sir," the nervous voice on the other end replied. "Uh, sir? Fleet command has broadcast that traitors and helots have taken over our vessel and the *Veritas*. They have ordered all available ships to destroy us both.

"What?" Marin shook his head. "Sound battle stations. Defend the ship. I'm returning to the bridge. Get the fleet admiral on the comm."

"There's a plot in motion, but no one on this ship is a part of it." Lucas shouted as the captain hurried past. "We're all pawns in this."

The captain paused and faced Lucas as if to say something.

Lucas pointed to the unconscious Magnus. "King Aelfric has been murdered and Prince Magnus kidnapped and left to die, but he lived. Magnus is our lawful king."

Over the vox system boomed the warning, "Incoming missiles. Brace for impact!"

Captain Marin pressed the ethercomm on his sleeve. "Magshield up!"

A boom rumbled through the ship.

Nearby, Captain Marin shouted into the ethercomm.

As Lucas lifted Katherine into his arms, a wave of nausea swept through him. The *Argonaut* had jumped.

They were on the way to Earth.

* * *

Recall the Earth is the second book in the Guardian Knights of Terra series. For more information about the series go to my website, www.KylePratt.me.

While you're there, sign up for my free author newsletter, and you'll be the first to know about my new books, discounts, and giveaways.

Thanks,
Kyle

Guardian Knights Lexicon

Aculeus stinger = The main personal weapon of the Valac. Unlike a scorpion, the stinger can be shot and quickly replaced by a new stinger.

Amplux = Laser.

Automatos = Automatic system. From the Greek meaning, "acting of itself." Any automatic system is said to be an automatos.

Auxilum = Sentient beings that have a centipede-like body. They are allies of the Mage. Auxilum is commonly shortened to "Aux."

Bioculus = Binoculars.

Computare = Computer.

Dart = A fast Terran planet-to-orbit shuttle. Depending upon the class, these are shuttle or deep space craft.

Curtana-class: high-value, long-range freighter

Espada-class: short-range surface-to-orbit personal transport

Rapier-class: armed military short-range fighter

Sabina-class: luxury mid-range personal transport

Sabre-class: armed military mid-range transport

Ethercomm = Transceiver (a radio) commonly shortened to "comm."

Geller = A light-year. Named after the Terran scientist that calculated it using Aux astronomical equipment.

Holoview = Holographic projector.

Helots = A subjugated population of humans (see "Seekers").

Lance = Gun/Rifle. A military lance has three modes of operation. In setting one, depending upon the model, it shoots bullets or shells (like a shotgun). In setting two, the lance fires a wireless electro-shock projectile something like a Taser. The third mode is an amplux (laser) beam.

Lingua Terra = The universal language of the Terran Kingdoms.

Magrail	= Magnetic Rail, similar to the magnetic levitation rail system.
Mage	= The overlords who provide the technology and coordinate the war against the Valac. Many commoners worship the Mage.
Mage Tunnel	= A wormhole.
Magshield	= Force field.
Medicus	= A military medic.
Monocular	= An optical instrument for viewing distant objects with one eye.
Palmcomp	= A handheld computer.
Seekers	= The Seekers of Earth, called helots by most people (see "Helot").
Skylift	= A space elevator.
Valac	= Scorpion-like sentient beings at war with the Mage, Auxilum and Terrans.
Vids	= Pictures or movies.
VidSet	= Television or video screen.
Vox	= A voice announcement system.
Wasp	= A Valac frighter craft.
Web	= A network of Computares or ethercomms.

Also by the Author

Titan Encounter Justin Garrett starts one morning as a respected business-man and ends the day a fugitive wanted by every power in the known universe. Fleeing with his 'sister' Mara and Naomi, a mysterious woman from Earth Empire, their only hope of refuge is with the Titans, genetically enhanced soldiers who rebelled, and murdered millions in the Titanomachy War. Hunted, even as they hunt for the Titans, the three companions slowly uncover the truth that will change the future and rewrite history.

* * *

Final Duty Twenty years after the death of her father during the Battle of Altair, Lieutenant Amy Palmer returns to the system as an officer aboard the recon-naissance ship Mirage. Almost imme-diately disaster strikes and Amy, along with the crew of the Mirage, must face the possibility of performing their final duties.

About the Author

Hello, and thank you for reading.

I grew up in the mountains of Colorado and went to Mesa State College in Grand Junction. When money for college ran low, I enlisted in the United States Navy. I thought I would do four years and then use my veteran's benefits to go back to college. Life often doesn't go as we plan it.

While serving in the navy, I wrote space opera and military science fiction stories. Both **Titan Encounter** and the **Final Duty** stories fall into that period.

My first assignment was with a U.S. Navy unit at the Royal Air Force base in Edzell, Scotland. Two years later, while on leave in Israel, I met Lorraine from Plymouth, Devon, England. We married the next year. Together we spent the remainder of my twenty-year naval career traveling across the United States from Virginia to Hawaii and on to Guam, Japan, and beyond.

After I retired from the military, I taught in an Alaskan Eskimo village for several years while continuing to write. My first post-apocalyptic novel, **Through Many Fires**, became an instant hit, rocketing onto the Kindle Science Fiction Post-Apocalyptic list and eventually making it to the number one spot. The second book in the series, *A Time to Endure*, appeared on several genre bestseller lists and led to the recently released third book in the series, **Braving the Storms.** My books are available on all major online retailers

Today, Lorraine and I live on a small farm in Western Washington State. You can learn more about me on my website, www.kylepratt.me.

If you like what you've read

I am an independent writer, so I don't have an advertising budget. If you've read one of my books and found it entertaining, please tell your friends. Also, the more favorable reviews a book has, the better it sells. So if you liked the story, please consider writing a review on the site where you downloaded this ebook. If you don't like the story, please tell me why.

About the Newsletter

Once a month I send out an email newsletter about upcoming books, events, specials, giveaways, promotions, and more—and I give a free ebook just for signing up! Sign up at www.kylepratt.me/contact/

I respect your privacy and will never rent, sell, or give away your personal information.